EVERY DAY
AFTER

EVERY DAY AFTER

Laura Golden

DELACORTE PRESS

Text copyright © 2013 by Laura Golden
Jacket art copyright © 2013 by Masterfile

All rights reserved. Published in the United States by Delacorte Press, an imprint of Random House Children's Books, a division of Random House, Inc., New York.

Delacorte Press is a registered trademark and the colophon is a trademark of Random House, Inc.

Grateful acknowledgment is made to Zondervan for permission to reprint the poem "Wits' End Corner" by Antoinette Wilson from *Streams in the Desert: 366 Daily Devotional Readings* by L. B. Cowman, copyright © 1996, 1997 by Zondervan. All rights reserved. Reprinted by permission of Zondervan.

Visit us on the Web! randomhouse.com/kids

Educators and librarians, for a variety of teaching tools, visit us at RHTeachersLibrarians.com

Library of Congress Cataloging-in-Publication Data
Golden, Laura.
Every day after / Laura Golden. — 1st ed.
p. cm.
Summary: "A young girl fights to keep her mama out of the mental ward, her home away from the bank, and herself out of the orphanage after her father abandons her and her mother in depression era Alabama"—Provided by publisher.
ISBN 978-0-385-74326-6 (hc) — ISBN 978-0-307-98312-1 (ebook) —
ISBN 978-0-375-99103-5 (glb)
[1. Self-reliance—Fiction. 2. Abandoned children—Fiction.
3. Family problems—Fiction. 4. Depressions—1929—Fiction.
5. Alabama—History—1819–1950—Fiction.] I. Title.
PZ7.G56474Ev 2013
[Fic]—dc23
2012015770

The text of this book is set in 11-point Excelsior.
Book design by Sarah Hoy

Printed in the United States of America
10 9 8 7 6 5 4 3 2 1

First Edition

*For Michael, who told me to write a
novel in the first place*

*And in memory of Jake and Nelda Perry—
one part Ben, one part Lizzie,
both deeply missed*

~ *One* ~

A Gem Is Not Polished Without Rubbing, nor a Man Perfected Without Trials

I learned a lot from my daddy, but the number one most important thing is this: never, ever, under any circumstances, let something get the best of you. To do this, you gotta work with what you got, play the cards you been dealt, turn lemons into lemonade. Too bad he wasn't around to see me doing just that, because one thing's for sure: when it rains in the South, it pours.

The late-April thunderstorm that had occurred overnight made my walk to school particularly interesting. Plodding a mile through red mud in shoes a size too small with four holes too many ain't the easiest thing to try. With the depression on, I wasn't the only one with this problem, but I might've been the only one who knew how to make the best of it. I'd turn lemons into lemonade by using Mother Nature's mess as an excuse not to worry about Daddy. Or Mama. I'd only worry about the mud, and how to get more of it. Instead of trying to keep it off my shoes, I'd see how much I could pack onto them. At least the cardboard cutouts inside would keep the bottoms of my socks from staining.

About every fifteen yards the mud would reach its highest clumping point and fall off. Maybe lighter steps would help it last longer.

A gruff voice broke my concentration. "Hey, Lizzie, wait up!"

"I was starting to wonder what'd happened to you," I said without turning around so I wouldn't break my mud.

I'd have known that voice anywhere. Ben's voice. I'd known him practically since birth. We were born within days of each other, and our mothers had once been best friends. Ben was my one true friend. I learned that over three years back, at the tail end of third grade. Myra Robinson had dared me to go up to crazy old Mr. Reed's and knock on his door. And that wasn't the worst of it. She expected me to talk to him. Me. Talk to a man older than the hills who probably hadn't said a hundred words since I'd been born. I figured if he'd felt like talking, he'd have talked, and I didn't care to be the one forcing him to do it.

I might not have been so nervous if Mr. Reed had been like any regular man and gone into town a good bit, or if he'd have darkened the doors of the Bittersweet Baptist Church at least on Easter Sundays. But Mr. Reed wasn't any regular man. He never went to church, and he headed into town exactly twice a month—on the first and the fifteenth from one p.m. till three p.m. But Myra had to go and dare me at precisely 3:17 p.m. on the eighth of March in the year 1929. Dang. He'd be home.

Ben had put his hand on my shoulder. "I'll go with you, Lizzie. I ain't scared."

Myra, along with about ten other nosy bystanders, trailed us into town. We turned off Main onto Oak Street, then onto Mr. Reed's rutted dirt drive, which led directly to his house up on the hill behind town. I didn't know about Ben, but I was as nervous as a long-tailed cat in a room full of rocking chairs. We tiptoed over the junk in the front yard—cracked mirrors, broken chairs, rusty pitchforks and hoes—and onto the sagging front porch. Daddy said Mr. Reed had lived alone for close to fifty years. I knew two things for certain: the house hadn't had a fresh coat of paint in all that time, and anything that broke got thrown out in the yard, not in the trash. Ben and I faced the splintered wooden door. He looked at me and nodded. I knocked. Slowly, the door creaked open, and there stood Mr. Reed, all leathery and wrinkled and thin as a bone.

He looked at us like *we* were the crazy ones. "What you kids need?" he asked. His voice was as rough as sandpaper. He put a cigarette to his mouth and took a long suck off it. Ben and I stood there blinking. Neither one of us knew what to say. We didn't need anything, except to get the heck out of there.

Ben was the one to find words. "Sorry to trouble ya, Mr. Reed. I don't reckon we need much of anything. We'll just be goin'."

Mr. Reed nodded and closed the door, and Ben and I took off like our tails were on fire.

"Did you do it?" Myra asked at the bottom of the hill. "What'd he say?"

"Yeah, we did it," I said. "And if you want to know, you go ask him yourself."

All the bystanders went abuzz, and Ben and I walked away. I could still hear my heart pounding in my ears. I'd never been gladder to have Ben by my side than I was that day. We'd been extra close ever since.

Now Ben walked beside me, staring down at my mud-covered shoes. "Sorry I'm late. Had to help Ma make the beds and clean the kitchen on top of my regular chores. What in the heck are you doin'?"

"Is she sick?" I asked, ignoring his question.

"Naw, she ain't sick. She's real busy tryin' to get a wedding quilt finished for Mrs. Martin's daughter. Mrs. Martin told Ma she needed it done by this evenin', nearly a week sooner than it was supposed to be due. Said she'd misfigured the time it'd take the postal service to get it out west to her daughter. Put Ma in a real hard spot."

I shook my head and sank into some soft mud. The clumps on my shoes grew. "I guess all those boarders living with her put her mind in a tizzy. The last few times I've gone to pick up some mending, she's either been in a

4

big hurry or snappy. Charlie told me he and John have to share their room with two other boys no more than five years old. If there was that many people crammed into my house, I'd probably have trouble thinking straight too."

Ben pulled a small rock from his pocket and placed it in his slingshot. Huge wads of mud covered my shoes. The weight nearly pulled them right off my feet. It was rather relaxing. Not up there with fishing or anything, but relaxing. Ben snapped his slingshot, and the rock smacked a pine.

"Why don't you teach me how to do that? Then we could have contests." I glanced over at him. "Contests I could win."

Ben pretended not to hear me. "I can't much blame Mrs. Martin either. A bunch of strangers stuffed in my house is the last thing I'd want."

I nudged Ben with my shoulder. "You're the one person who wouldn't wear me thin."

"No, Lizzie, I'm the only person *you* can't wear thin."

I reared back my fist, and if Ben hadn't been Ben, I would've let it fly. He held up his hands in surrender. I'm a girl, but I sure as heck don't hit like one, and Ben knew it. I stomped the mud off my shoes instead.

"I surely hope Ma finds a way to finish that quilt. Mrs. Martin's supposed to give her five dollars for it. Without it, we're likely gonna miss the mortgage again this month. Course, even with that money, making it still ain't a sure bet." The right corner of Ben's mouth retreated into his plump cheek. That meant one thing and one thing only: he was worried about something and he didn't want to yap on and on about it. I let him be.

Mud squished beneath our feet and leaves rustled in the breeze. I tried my hardest not to think of Daddy in the quiet, but I couldn't help it. I couldn't help wondering why he had to go, and why he hadn't said good-bye.

It was little more than a month since he'd left, but it might as well have been an eternity. I didn't know how much longer me and Mama could last without him. Like Ben, I'd already opened one overdue mortgage bill since Daddy left, but I felt sure he wasn't gonna let me open another. He'd be back in time to save us from the bank. He had to.

I clutched my gold locket, rubbing its rough lines of engraving with my thumb: ELIZABETH CLAIRE HAWKINS 1876. Elizabeth Claire Hawkins—Daddy's mama and my namesake. Daddy had shown me the locket only a few times over the years, but I'd memorized it the first time I'd laid eyes on it: a shiny golden oval with a face of delicate loops and swirls. Inside were tiny portraits of Grandmother and Grandfather wearing their most serious faces.

The locket was meant for my eighteenth birthday. Daddy said I had to earn it by growing into a fearless young woman worthy of the Hawkins name—just like Grandma. Well, it wasn't my eighteenth birthday, and I was toting around more than a pound of fear, but here was the locket dangling from my neck. I'd inherited it a little over six years too soon, on the morning Daddy disappeared. He'd left a note for Mama, the locket for me. He didn't have to tell me what it meant to get it early. I knew. He was telling me it was time to prove my worth, and he expected me to do it by passing the hardest of tests: I had to hold everything together until he came home. I couldn't let him down.

Daddy had replaced the pictures of Grandmother and Grandfather, and I pictured the two faces now tucked inside—one wrinkled and weathered from thirty-seven years on this earth, the other much smoother, much younger. Both heads were topped with white-blond hair so thin light shone right through it. Mama always said Daddy and me didn't have hair, we had down.

Ben let out a soft whistle beside me. I looked at him. His face had relaxed. We were the same, Ben and me, both trying our hardest not to think about having to play the cards we'd been dealt. We knew they weren't good hands, and it wasn't fair. He let one last rock fly, then stuffed his slingshot into his back pocket as we entered the schoolyard.

~ *Two* ~

After Honour and State
Follow Envy and Hate

Nearly every student older than six was out in front of the school. The older ones stood talking in their usual groups of three or four; the youngest took turns sliding down the smooth boulders jutting up from the ground beside the school. Only two or three of the shyest were already making their way inside.

I pulled off my shoes and scraped them through the grass. Clumped mud smeared across the ground. I couldn't get the shoes perfectly clean, but I reckoned I'd known that before I'd started trying. I put them back on and followed Ben as we ducked and dodged around the groups. I spotted Erin Sawyer peering at us from around Scott McClain's blubbery belly. His massive body, the largest in school and him only an eighth grader, dwarfed Erin's tiny one.

"Excuse us," Ben mumbled to the dirt as he edged past Scott on his way over to Erin.

I refused to excuse myself to a blamed brat, especially one who made a never-ending habit of calling my daddy a hobo. I'd already taught him a lesson once, and he could bet his last nickel I'd do it again. I scowled as I passed. To my delight, Scott grabbed his swollen nose and retreated.

That was one bully down, one left to go. Erin stood there staring, her arms folded tightly across her chest. Wasn't nothin' new. She'd hated most everyone around here from the time she'd showed up in Bittersweet back in August. She'd arrived complete with her lawyer daddy and know-it-all mother. They'd come over from Georgia. Mr. Sawyer had told Daddy that law work wasn't any good over there, but I didn't see how a tiny town like Bittersweet would be much different. Even Dr. Heimler had been forced to shut down his office and work from his house. I figured if there wasn't enough money to pay the town doctor, there sure wasn't enough to pay for a new lawyer, and the Sawyers needed to go on back where they came from.

It wouldn't have been a big loss. About the only kid who liked Erin was Ben. He'd always gone out of his way to be nice to her, even when he shouldn't have. But then again, I'd never actually seen Ben be mean to anyone or anything. He wouldn't even do in a rattlesnake we once found in his barn, coiled up and rattling in front of a bale of hay. When I told him to whack it with a shovel, he refused. "That rattler's one of God's creatures too. It'll leave when it's ready." A couple of hours later, it slithered away.

I figured if Ben could like a rattlesnake, it was entirely possible for him to like Erin, 'cause there was no denying she was just as mean as one.

"Hey, Erin," Ben said, shoving his hands deep inside his pockets. By the way he was acting, you'd think Erin Sawyer was the prettiest thing in all God's creation. While she wasn't ugly on the outside, I could assure Ben her insides didn't match.

Erin wouldn't look at Ben. She was too busy scowling at me. Her eyes squinted into slits behind her glasses. Her fists balled, turning her knuckles white.

"What'd I do now?" I asked, though I already knew. But why should I give her what she wanted? She'd still be mad all the time anyway, and she couldn't hurt me.

"What you always do. Acted like the selfish person you are."

Ben placed his hand on her shoulder in typical peacemaker fashion. "Just calm down and tell Lizzie why you're upset."

"I will not tell her, because she knows," Erin snapped. Her eyes had gone from slits to saucers, and the way her glasses magnified them, I was afraid they might pop out.

"I'm going inside," I said. "I'm tired of this."

But instead of walking inside, I landed facedown on the ground, the musty smell of mud drifting up my nose.

"You ain't gotta trip her, Erin," said Ben, reaching to help me up.

"You stay out of this, Ben." Erin glared at me. She

pointed at my face. "I'm through playing games with you, Lizzie. I'm gonna give you one last chance to take your name off that list."

I stood and tried to brush the mud from the front of my dress. I figured Erin was ready to wring my neck 'cause I'd gone off and signed up for the essay contest Miss Jones ran for the sixth-grade class twice each term. The winner received extra points toward their final grade. After I'd won the last three contests, Erin had been at me about this one. I'd come in first place with the highest grades last term. She'd come in second. She couldn't stand it. She probably thought if she could win the extra credit, it'd give her enough to beat me out at the end of this term. Well, I wasn't about to let that happen. I had to hold on to my top spot for Daddy, and I needed those extra points to do it. More than ever. "It's a free country, Erin. I've got just as much right to be in that contest as you. I like to keep my grades in top shape. Daddy always told me getting good grades is my most important job."

"Your *daddy* told you!" She laughed. "You may not have noticed, but your daddy's gone."

I should've let her words roll off me like water off a duck's feathers, but I didn't. I couldn't. "He'll be back, and I'll have the grades he'll expect to see." The words poured out smooth and easy, like warm honey. "I wouldn't pull out of that essay contest now if it was your dying wish. It's too much fun beating you."

Erin's fair skin flushed deep red. There was no doubt

about it: her eyes were coming out. "You don't need that extra credit, Lizzie Hawkins, and you know it. You just can't stand the thought of somebody else winning. Now take your name off that list. I know I can win it without you entering, and that's exactly what I aim to do." She peered over the rim of her glasses. "Everybody around here, including me, knows you're Miss Jones's little pet, and if your essay is in that contest, nobody else stands a chance."

Now, truth be told, I'd have been more than happy to be Miss Jones's little pet, but fact was fact. I worked hard for everything I got. Miss Jones had never given me any special privileges. Just Friday past, I'd received three whacks on my palm with a hickory switch for bloodying Scott McClain's nose during recess. Pets do not get punished. Erin seemed to have forgotten that.

"I'm warning you to drop out, Lizzie. It's not fair. I'm sick to death of watching you win everything. If you do it, I'll stop bothering you."

She wouldn't be satisfied till I dropped out, but Daddy said quitting made you look weak. Anyway, the chances of her calling a truce with me were slim. I had a better chance of becoming the next Greta Garbo. She just wanted to taste sweet victory for herself. And I knew how that worked. She'd get one lick and then she'd be hungry for more. One win is never enough.

Besides, although I wasn't about to let anyone else know it, I needed that extra credit. Badly. I'd been able to hold on to the top grades in my class for nearly two years straight, even before Erin showed up. But now, with Daddy gone and Mama sick, I didn't have so much time to study anymore. My study time was mostly spent mending clothes for extra money or tending to chores, and my grades were beginning to take a small hit. I felt a pang of doubt that I could finish my essay by May ninth. I hadn't even started it yet. But I refused to give up.

I looked at Erin like I might be considering her offer. I wasn't. "You don't know *how* to stop bothering me," I said. "I haven't dropped out before, and I'm not about to start now, so I guess you'll just have to get over all your jealousy."

Erin stood there gaping. Ben didn't look much different. The schoolyard was now deserted except for a few stragglers staring in our direction. Erin was more than aware of the eavesdroppers and huffed, "Jealous? What's there to be jealous of? You've got nothing but a hobo daddy and a loony mother."

A flurry of gasps and giggles erupted from the surrounding spies. Ben grabbed ahold of Erin's arm, attempting to hush her up. She jerked away. Her eyes flickered. "You're in a bad way, and you know it. You know what happens to kids when their parents can't take care of them? They get carted off to the nearest orphanage, that's what. I'd hate for that to happen to you. Course, if it did, I guess I wouldn't have to put up with you hogging the spotlight all the time, would I?"

I yanked Erin close. Her muscles tensed beneath my grip. "You threatening me, Erin Sawyer? Because I've got news for you: I'm not going anywhere. You don't have any idea what you're talking about. Daddy's off finding work and Mama is fine. She's just real busy with Daddy gone, that's all."

Truthfully, Mama wasn't fine. It was a good day if she knew I existed. And Daddy hadn't yet filled us in on exactly where his travels had taken him, but Erin didn't know that, and she wasn't going to. Yep, when it rains in Alabama, it pours, and sometimes you gotta work with what you got. Well, all I had to work with were fibs.

Miss Jones appeared in the doorway. "Come along, children. We don't have all day."

Erin stomped off. Ben grabbed my arm and pulled me inside. He whispered something in my ear, but all I could hear was Mama quoting from her book of proverbs and sayings Daddy had given her before I was born: "After honour and state follow envy and hate." I'd never gotten it before, but I did now. I got it good.

Inside, Erin took her usual seat behind me. It was nearly too much to bear, having to sit with the back of my desk permanently attached to the front of hers. How was I supposed to make lemonade from that? She leaned forward, her hot breath blowing past my ear. As the door clicked shut she whispered, "I've had it with you, Lizzie Hawkins, and I'm gonna make you pay."

~ *Three* ~

He Who Would Gather Roses
Must Not Fear Thorns

By the time school was dismissed, the sun had come out in full force. Its heat had turned the mud puddles to sticky holes in the road. Wind wisped through the oaks and ruffled the honeysuckle vines overtaking Mr. Watson's pasture fence. Ben pulled a pebble from his pocket and placed it in his slingshot. *Snap!* A sharp crack ricocheted off a bare post. Ben's dad had given him that slingshot for his eighth birthday. He'd always loved it, but during the past year, since Mr. Butler had passed away, Ben hadn't let that slingshot out of his sight. I suspected he even slept with it, like a baby with a blanket.

I watched him cradle it in his tanned hands. He was too quiet after Erin's threat. He hadn't said a single word since we'd left school. I couldn't stand his calm any longer. "Did you see the looks she kept giving me? So my grades are better than hers. That's no reason to have me packed off to an orphanage. And I still can't figure exactly how she knows about Mama. You think she's heard it from all the church ladies?"

Ben scratched his neck and kicked a rock across the road. He popped his slingshot's empty band. Of all the times for him to get quiet, why did it have to be now? I stomped a ball of dried mud, crushing it into a thousand tiny particles. I was mad, and I wanted Ben to be angry too. But he wasn't. He was too busy popping and snapping that blasted band.

"Those church ladies probably think Mama's crazy for not coming to church lately. A few of 'em came by to visit after Daddy left, to drop off a jar of jam or a batch of biscuits, but they never saw Mama. I always told 'em she was scrubbing floors or gone into town. They never seemed to doubt me. But still, when they stopped showing, their mouths likely started moving. Do you figure that's where Erin heard it?"

Ben shrugged and cleared his throat like he was gonna say something. He didn't.

"Benjamin Butler!" I yelled. "Do you hear me?"

It was times like these I'd have traded Ben for a girl in a blink. Girls live to get riled up over stuff. Boys would shake hands with the man who'd shot their dog.

He snatched up a rock and shot it into a sweet gum. A single leaf floated to the ground. "I just got a lot on my mind."

"Good. You should. I was starting to think you didn't care what Erin did to me."

"Course I care, Lizzie. That's why I think you should just sit this contest out. You've probably got the best grades anyway."

"And I'd like to keep it that way. Extra credit is sorta like my guarantee. And there's no point in feeling sorry for Erin. You know her. What she wants, she gets."

Ben raked his fingers through his straw-colored hair. "Sounds like somebody else around here."

I heaved a breath in frustration. Ben wasn't as worried about me as he should've been. Heck, he didn't seem worried at all. But then again, he always wanted to see the best in people. He even refused to believe it was Erin who'd scared the life out of Myra Robinson. The very same Myra Robinson who'd dared me to knock at Mr. Reed's door.

It happened last October, not two months after Erin came to Bittersweet. Erin and Myra had started out friends, but Erin didn't realize that she'd gone off and picked the wrong girl to friend up with—a bully just like herself. Aside from whipping out dares faster than green grass passes through a goose, Myra had the nasty little habit of spreading rumors, and it wasn't long before she was spreading one about Erin. One Friday morning, Myra began swearing up one side and down the other that Erin was adopted. I didn't know whether to believe it, but the Sawyers were pretty old. Not grandparent old or anything, but older than everyone else's parents. And Erin didn't look a thing like either of them, except for her eyes. You could've plucked out Mr. Sawyer's eyes, put them in Erin, and not been able to tell the difference. And anyway, why would they want to hide that Erin was adopted?

Well, by Monday afternoon, Erin had got wind of what Myra was telling the whole school. That Thursday, just as me and Ben were about to split an ice-cold Nehi from Hinkle's General Store, Ziggy got loose. It was a known fact that Myra Robinson was terrified of dogs. Huge or tiny, old or young, it didn't matter. If it had four legs and barked, she ran the other way. It was also a known fact that each afternoon Myra had to run past Mr. Reed's driveway on her way home from school.

Besides holding the prize for Town Resident Older than Dirt, Mr. Reed also claimed bragging rights for Owner of the Friskiest Dog in All Creation. Ziggy, Mr. Reed's pampered retriever, would find a way to move even if you glued his paws to the ground. He's kept penned at all times, except for the occasional squirrel- or duck-hunting trip, because he knocks down every poor soul who crosses his path. He'd never once gotten out of his pen until that very moment when Myra happened to be running past.

Ziggy never could resist a moving target. He bolted and headed straight down the hill, right toward Myra. She went to screaming like she was dying, squealing so loud she almost cracked a window at Hinkle's. She headed for the nearest door, but Ziggy was too fast for her. He jumped up and she went down, kicking and screaming something fierce. Mr. Hinkle rushed out and pulled Ziggy off her. Myra took off like a burglar from a bank, her back soaked with dog slobber. A muddy puddle marked the place where she'd gone down, and the front of her departing dress told where that puddle had come from. She'd flat out wet herself! Right there in front of God and everybody.

Soon enough the whole school was talking about it. Eliza Dawson, the sheriff's daughter, had been walking to the sheriff's office and had seen the whole thing too, and everybody knows a sheriff's daughter isn't allowed to exaggerate. No one ever figured out how Ziggy got loose, but I knew. Myra Robinson knew too, but she wasn't about to tattle on Erin for fear the next act of revenge would be even worse. Myra went the long way home from then on.

The Robinsons moved to Huntsville just before Christmas, and some say it was because of what happened with Ziggy. No kid had dared say the word "adopted" or cross Erin in any other way since . . . until me. I had no doubt she was planning her revenge, but I wasn't about to give her the satisfaction of carrying it out. She was barking up the wrong tree.

I looked over at Ben. His mouth was moving, but I only heard the last of what he was saying. ". . . somehow. You know?"

I stared at him, not sure how I was supposed to answer. "Uh-huh" was all that came out.

"You weren't listening again, were you?"

"I was listening," I said in my most convincing voice. "I just didn't quite catch that last part."

"Forget it," he mumbled. "We goin' fishin' today or not?"

"Yep. I just need to check on Mama and change first. You run on and grab the poles. I'll meet you down there."

"All right," he said. "Hurry." He took off toward our barn.

I bounded onto the front porch, kicked off my crusty shoes, and ran inside. "Mama, I'm home," I called. There was no reply. Before Daddy left, Mama would answer with "Hey, sweet. Did you have a good day?" But every day after, I'd been greeted only by silence.

I peeked through the curtain at the back porch. She was in her rocker, the exact spot I'd left her when I headed off to school. She'd need to stand up and stretch her legs, and I'd have to make her do it. Otherwise, she'd rock in that chair till the rails fell off.

I ran into my room and changed as quickly as I could—T-shirt and overalls, bare feet. Prime fishing wear. I threw my mud-stained dress into the bag with the rest of the clothes I needed to wash. The dress would need to be scrubbed harder than usual, and even then the stain was probably set already. My church dress would have to do for school until next laundry day. My crusty shoes could be cleaned off down at the pond.

I hurried to the icebox and chipped some ice off the block—one chip for me, the rest in a glass of water for Mama. I took it out to her.

She didn't look up. She never did. She just sat there, staring, her right hand resting in her lap, clutching her worn book of old proverbs. Mama had become quiet over the past month. Too quiet. She was no longer feisty, no longer sharply spouting off the exact right quote from her book at the exact right time, no longer racing me down to the pond to fish with Daddy. Those parts of her had disappeared with Daddy. She didn't laugh anymore or cry anymore. She simply *was*.

I held the glass up to her. "Are you thirsty, Mama? I brought you some water."

She took the teeniest sip. I set the glass on the wooden table beside her rocker, then reached down and took her hand. It was bony and frail, yet warm and comforting at the same time. She rocked in steady rhythm. Loose strands of graying hair wisped across her sunken cheeks, escapees from the tight bun I'd made earlier at the base of her neck. Mama's looks had always been soft and lady-like, but lately they'd developed an aged hardness that shook me down deep.

I helped her up, still grasping her hand. "Want to walk a little?"

She gripped my hand with one of hers, still tightly clutching her book with the other. We strolled back and forth across the porch, my arm hooked into hers. After a few minutes, she began to pull at me. She needed to rest.

I eased her back into the rocker and glanced at the pond. Ben was already down there. I pointed him out to

Mama. "Me and Ben are going fishing down at the pond. You can watch us if you want."

Nothing.

"Wish us luck," I said. "I'll be back in a bit to fix supper."

I went out through the front door to grab my shoes, then headed around back into the field. Fishing after school had become more than a habit; it was a need. At least, it was for me. Before Daddy left, I'd fished with him almost daily, except during winter, when fishing wasn't good anyway. To me, fishing was the best thing in the world, and I didn't understand girls who spent their time on pointless activities like primping or gabbing on and on about boys.

I spotted Ben's boots lying in the grass and smiled at my own bare feet. We always fished barefooted. It's an unspoken rule in Bittersweet—if you ain't barefooted, you ain't fishing. The cool grass tickled my toes, and the still-damp ground sank with each step.

I glanced back at Mama rocking away on the porch. I waved. She didn't. I squatted down in the grass beside Ben and began to rinse my shoes in the warm, shallow water. Orangey mud swirled into the pond. "You think she'll ever wave back again?"

Ben stopped digging and dropped another worm into his carton. "One day. Just that nobody knows when."

I sat my shoes beside my pole, plopped down beside them, and hugged my knees to my chest. Though Ben was trying his best, he couldn't hide his true thoughts from me. We both knew that as long as Daddy stayed gone, so would she. Erin hadn't seen Mama since Daddy left, and I had to keep it that way. The minute she saw her would be the minute I was hauled off to the nearest orphanage and Mama to the nearest mental ward.

"What if she never does? What if I can't get her back? The biggest things I've done up till now are making As and catching old One-Eye. That's it. And I had Daddy here on both counts. Now, not only do I have to make sure we don't get booted from our house, I have to take care of Mama too. I'd give anything for Daddy to come home. This must be what it feels like at Wits' End Corner."

"Where?" Ben rumpled his brows. "I ain't heard of that before."

I lay back on the soft ground. "It's a poem Mama's had for a while. I forgot where she found it, and I don't remember all of it, but I like it."

"What part do you remember?"

"Only the first lines, but I can say them if you want to hear."

Ben scooted closer to me.

I cleared my throat and tried to make the words as flowing and beautiful as Mama did:

> *"Are you standing at 'Wits' End Corner,'*
> *Christian, with a troubled brow?*

Are you thinking of what is before you,
And all you are bearing now?
Does all the world seem against you,
And you in the battle alone?
Remember—at 'Wits' End Corner'
Is just where God's power is shown."

I must've done Mama proud with my voice, because Ben sat silent for a few seconds after I finished. He nodded slowly. "I like it," he said. "I wish you knew the rest."

"Me too. Maybe I can find it later. Anyway, that's pretty much how I feel, but if God's gonna show His power, I wish He'd hurry up and do it already. Me and Mama need Daddy back home."

"Awww, Lizzie. I know you want your daddy here, but you'll make it till he comes back."

Ben stood and dusted the seat of his britches. He grabbed his slingshot and began mindlessly snapping the band. I pulled at the grass waiting for *the* snap—the snap that came along with some brilliant idea. Well, brilliant coming from Ben.

A few minutes of peace later—*SNAP!* "I got it!" he yelled, his near invisible brows shooting high up his freckled forehead. He snatched my pole off the ground and shoved it into my hands. "Catch him," he commanded.

I eyed Ben, trying to understand what he meant.

"Don't sit there like a blasted block of ice. Catch him. Catch ol' One-Eye. Ain't a soul ever caught that fish but

24

you, Lizzie Hawkins, not even your daddy. Do everything you did before, even though he ain't here this time. If you can do that, you can do anything."

"That's crazy. That won't tell me anything."

Ben smiled. "Sure it will. Kinda like a sign. I never did tell ya what happened the first time I had to plow after Pa passed. I was too embarrassed to say anything, but it'll show ya what I mean."

I nodded.

"Well, I was pretty nervous. I was worried to death that ol' Jack'd take off and drag me behind the plow or, even worse, that I couldn't get him hitched up in the first place. So I put an old tin can up on a fence post, pulled out my slingshot, and told myself if I shot that can off ten times in a row from a fair distance, I could plow without Pa. I figured shootin' that can would be harder than plowing."

I eased in closer to Ben. "Did you do it?"

"Sure did. Pretty as you please."

"Did you get the field plowed?"

"Oh, I got the field plowed, all right, but . . ." Ben's smile faded.

"Well, you gonna tell me or not?"

He cleared his throat and mumbled, "I plowed off my big toenail doing it."

I jumped up from my cozy spot in the grass. "Ben! So that's why you fished with your shoes on back then. Why didn't you just tell me that before when I asked? And what are you saying now? That I'll catch One-Eye again, but I'll end up with a hook jabbed through my finger?"

"No, I ain't sayin' that. Look, I did it, didn't I? Shootin' the can was a test. That's what this is for you—a test. Can't hurt to try."

I was shocked at myself for believing Ben's fiddle-faddle enough to try it, but it sounded right. If I could catch that fish again without Daddy here, I was nearly certain I could do whatever else I set my mind to, including keeping myself out of the orphanage and Mama safe. Then I'd be able to leave Wits' End Corner once and for all. It might sound pretty in a poem, but it surely was not a fun place to be.

I clutched my locket and pictured Daddy's face. *Please, God,* I begged. *Please let me pass this test.*

~ Four ~

Luck Follows the Hopeful,
Ill Luck the Fearful

I leaned my head back, feeling the warmth of the sun. I squeezed my eyes tight. Colors and light flashed beneath my eyelids. Gradually, the colors became shapes and the shapes became people, forming clear images of me and Daddy on that muggy morning last August.

Daddy insisted it was too hot to fish, but I wouldn't listen. Christmas, candy, even Goo Goo Clusters paled in comparison to fishing with Daddy, and a little heat wasn't gonna stop me.

"Please. Just for an hour," I begged. "The fish'd be good for supper."

"Oh, all right, Lizzie." He propped his hoe against the side of the house and sopped his face with his sleeve. "You get the bait; I'll grab the poles."

I rushed into the barn for the worms. Mama could get pretty riled up when she wanted something done and didn't get it, and that day she wanted her vegetable garden weeded. If Daddy didn't leave within five minutes, he'd start thinking about the trouble he'd be in when he got back. We were gone within three, tromping through the field to the pond behind our house.

The sweet scent of hay mingled in the air with the pungent smell of freshly plowed dirt, but Daddy didn't seem to notice. His steps were heavy, his jaw tight. He reminded me of the man in *Pilgrim's Progress,* carrying his heavy burdens and not knowing how to let them go.

All my life Daddy had been willful and full of fire, but he'd changed the day he lost his job at the steel mill. Seemed to me a lot of folks around town had lost their jobs since the depression came on back in '29. I guess Daddy had figured he might skirt by. That wasn't in his cards. He'd been laid off a month and a half earlier, and I'd begun to wonder if he'd ever be his old self again.

"You wait. I'm gonna land the biggest fish yet," I said when we reached the pond. I shielded the sun from my eyes and studied the water.

"Maybe," said Daddy, only half listening. "Now hand me those worms and bait up."

As usual, he was the first to land a fish. He was always first at everything. He tossed it back into the water and it darted away. "That's one," he said, holding up his pointer finger.

I shook my head. "Uh-uh. That puny bream didn't count. He was even too little to keep."

I jumped up from my fishing spot and jogged out into

the field. On hands and knees I dug and poked through freshly cut hay.

"What on earth are you doing?" Daddy called as he hooked another worm. "You won't catch anything out there."

"I'm finding a cricket. We only ever fish with worms and neither of us has caught him yet. Maybe he's a picky eater."

"Caught who?"

"One-Eye."

Daddy shook his head. "Uh-uh-uh." He cast out his line.

Five minutes later, a juicy cricket dangled from my hook. I tossed it into the water and sat stone still. The only movement came from my heart. Each time it beat, my hands jerked a little. I focused on the motion, trying hard to keep it from happening. Up-down my hands went in barely noticeable rhythm. Up-down, up-down, *OUT!*

"I got one!" I shrieked. For a moment, I thought I might've hooked a whale. Every muscle in my body, from my toes to my eyeballs, tensed in resistance to the fish's pulls and jerks. The pole dug into my hands.

Moving faster than he had in weeks, Daddy jumped up to encourage me. "Hold 'im, Lizzie. He's a real fighter. If you want to see him, you're gonna have to beat him." He propped his lanky hands on his knees, straining for a glimpse of the fish as it slapped and splashed in the water.

I took a deep breath and dug way down deep, deeper

29

than I ever had, and just like Daddy told me to do, I fought that fish. After one last glorious heave, the fish slid onto land.

"Oh, my Lord," said Daddy, his eyes bigger than Grandfather's pocket watch. He stared at the conquered catfish as it squirmed in the grass. It had only one eye.

"It's him," I uttered. "One-Eye."

Town legend had told of a one-eyed channel cat living in our pond for more than fifty years. Folks were said to have seen him skimming old bait or bread crumbs off the top of the water, but no one had ever actually caught him. Ben and I had always believed One-Eye existed, but Daddy had insisted the story held as much water as a busted glass. After all, anyone worth his salt knew catfish didn't live that long, and Daddy had never seen him, and it was *his* pond. Mama said sometimes folks see what they want to see, even if it's not there.

But Daddy and I weren't seeing things now. One-Eye was real, as real as could be, and longer than Daddy's lower leg. I slid my fingers across the perfect smoothness of his charcoal-colored body. He squirmed faster in protest.

"I can't believe it," Daddy hollered. "He's real! My own Lizzie Girl just landed ol' One-Eye!"

My own Lizzie Girl. The words hung in the air for a second, then seeped into my soul. Daddy had called me that only a few times in my life. He saved it for those occasions when I made him extra proud, when he felt like bragging that I was his.

Daddy stood hunched over the catfish with his mouth gaping as though he was gonna say something. Nothing came out. He tipped his hat back off his forehead, revealing the beaded sweat above his brows. For once he didn't wipe it away.

My spirits soared right with his. I hoped the feeling would last, more for Daddy than for me. I'd never seen him as down as he'd been over the last month and a half. He'd even taken to mentioning leaving to find work. Mama didn't like that talk one bit. She'd either get real upset or real quiet. One was as bad as the other. But maybe if Daddy stayed happy, he wouldn't leave, and Mama wouldn't be upset, and everything could go back to normal again. Maybe.

Daddy rubbed his whiskered chin and grinned. "Wanna keep 'im?"

I could see him sizing up the bragging rights he'd have if we kept him. For Daddy, this was the win of the century, and without the carcass to prove it, no one would believe that I, beanpole Lizzie Hawkins, had actually caught ol' One-Eye.

One-Eye squirmed on the ground, gasping for air. He was switching back and forth faster now, attempting to find the water. He couldn't run away, but he wasn't about to stop trying. Daddy was right—he was a fighter.

He'd been born to win, to survive. Just like Daddy. Just like me.

"Let's let him go," I said. "A fighter like him should be free. Besides, I want to see if anyone else can catch him. Maybe I outsmarted him, or maybe he's just going a little cuckoo in his old age."

Daddy looked at me, his dark eyes hard and squinted. "You sure? You might not catch him again."

I shrugged. "Let him go."

We watched in silence as One-Eye slid back into the water. Unlike the skittish bream Daddy had hooked earlier, One-Eye lingered near the shore for a few seconds before slinking off into the deep. It was as if he was saluting me for being a worthy, and merciful, opponent. On the inside, I saluted him, too.

We caught five more fish between us that day. They made some fine fried fish for supper, and Mama gave me the best piece as a reward for my accomplishment. But as good as that fish tasted, I was prouder of One-Eye. I'd caught the best that could be caught in our pond, possibly the best that could be caught in the whole state of Alabama. Once Daddy had spread the story around town, he had more people than ever asking to fish at our pond. He and a few others tried their hardest to land ol' One-Eye again, but no one did. After a couple of weeks, people began to doubt it'd really been ol' One-Eye I'd caught after all.

Ben shoved me, forcing my eyes open. "You gonna try

it or not? 'Cause if you ain't, I got better things to do than sit around here watching you sleep."

"I'm going. I just needed a little inspiration, that's all."

"Well, you're takin' way too long gettin' it. Ain't no sense in puttin' it off."

"I'm not putting it off. Watch."

I stomped through the grass to the exact spot I had been at on that day and began to dig. Confidence pulsed through my body. It was me who'd caught One-Eye. Daddy hadn't done a thing. He hadn't told me to use a cricket, and he sure as heck hadn't helped me reel him in. Maybe I was just being childish about needing Daddy, like someone needing a teddy bear or a blanket. Ben was right. I could do it again.

Before long I was marching back to the pond with another fat cricket hanging from my hook. I tossed the line into the water and waited. And waited. And waited. I watched my hands bobbing up and down for good measure.

"How long did it take you before?" asked Ben as he tossed his freshly baited line into the water.

I glared at him. "Not this long, but then again, I didn't have an all-fired pest sitting right next to me either." I reeled in my line. "Ha!" I said, waving the empty hook in Ben's face. "Those blasted bream don't know how to leave your bait alone."

Back out in the field, I pretended to be calm, but a small cloud of doubt had formed. It's funny how you can be sure of yourself one minute, then doubt yourself the next, but that is exactly what one little bream made me do.

Twice more I repeated the process. Bait, line, wait. And wait. And wait.

"I think you oughta check your line again," said Ben after stringing up his third bream.

Again I reeled in my line. The cricket remained. I had to face facts: The cricket wasn't missing. Daddy was.

The cloud that had been growing bigger by the minute burst into a furious storm inside my head. Ben tried to comfort me, but I couldn't hear his words. I was straining to hear Daddy's: *You're a Hawkins, Lizzie Girl. A true one. You were put on this earth for a reason—to fight and to win. Don't ever forget it. I know you won't let me down.*

Born to succeed? Yes. But was I born to succeed without him? I wasn't so sure.

~ *Five* ~

Heaven Is at the Feet of Mothers

Please, Lord, not again!

Sleep laughed at me, poked at me, refused to come. And when I thought I'd beaten it, it brought nightmares— nightmares about failure, and loss, and loneliness.

Since Daddy had gone, night after night had ended with me wide-eyed and balled up like a baby beneath a rumpled pile of scratchy sheets. Though I couldn't force sleep to come, I had to try. I couldn't help myself.

Mama said I'd been stubborn like that even before I was born. The doctors had told her many times she'd never have a baby; just the way God made her. Daddy said I proved 'em wrong. I fought my way into existence, and on a mild night in May of 1920, I fought my way into this world. I hadn't stopped fighting since.

I rolled over and squinted at my clock, trying to make out the time. Ten till five. *Ugh!* It'd be another whole hour before I needed to wake Mama.

I'd been fighting all night. There wasn't any sense in

whipping a dead horse. I threw back my covers, shuffled over to my dresser, and rummaged past the clutter in the bottom drawer: photos of me with Ben last Easter, wads of single socks, and two crumpled brown paper bags that still held the scent of long-ago-eaten Goo Goo Clusters. Beneath the jumble lay the leather-bound journal Mama had given me for my last birthday.

"You'll know when it's time to write," she'd said.

She was right. I did know. I knew the morning Daddy disappeared. It was the only thing I'd written so far—an entry dated March 30, 1932. After I wrote about Daddy leaving, I couldn't stand to look at the journal anymore. I'd stuffed it into the bottom dresser drawer and hadn't touched it since. The feelings I felt on that morning were trapped inside the journal, and I wanted to push them away. If I cracked open the journal's cover, all that hurt and pain might come rushing back inside me. But the fear of failure had built up too high. I couldn't help it. I had to let it spill out.

I held the journal in my hands, feeling the smooth leather cover and the weight of the words under it. I closed my eyes and promised myself I wouldn't peek at that first entry. Then all that pain would stay where it belonged—on the page.

Eyes still closed, I opened the cover and counted three pages in, just to be safe. I opened my eyes and looked at the clean white page before me. My pencil drifted onto the sheet and I let the words flow.

April 29, 1932

I went fishing with Ben today. He told me to catch One-Eye again. He said it'd prove I could do anything I set my mind to, like taking care of Mama and keeping everything in order. I failed. I know Daddy would be disappointed in me, not just about One-Eye, but about my grades too. They're not bad, but they're dropping. I just don't have enough time to study anymore. It'll be a miracle if I can hold on to my top spot in class. If I don't, it'll kill Daddy.

I can't let him down. Anytime I do, I feel just as bad as I did the first time I disappointed him. Even though I was only seven, I remember it plain as day.

Thunder boomed and lightning flashed outside, but I wasn't scared. I was brave, staying in my room to play with the Humpty Dumpty Circus I'd gotten the Christmas before.

A heavy clap of thunder rattled the windows. Mama called to me from the parlor, "Lizzie, you want to come sit with me?"

"No, ma'am. I'm not scared."

"That's my girl," Daddy called back. "You see," he said to Mama, "what a brave girl we have. You tell me of any other little girl—or boy, for that matter—who'd sit alone through a storm like this."

I puffed up like a toad at hearing that. I was

*brave. But I'd gotten too puffed up too soon. A
few seconds later, a blinding flash of lightning cut
through the darkness outside, followed by a boom
loud enough to wake the dead. The lights in the
house flickered and my room went dark. Pitch
dark. I couldn't see my hands in front of my face.
My skin turned to gooseflesh and the hairs on the
back of my neck pricked up. I imagined bony ghost
fingers reaching out through the blackness and
grabbing me.*

*"Maaaammmaaaa!" I screamed. Until then, I
didn't know I could squeal that loud.*

*"I'm coming, baby," Mama answered. "I'm
coming."*

*Light flooded into the room as Mama entered
with her kerosene lantern. She reached down,
took my hand, and led me into the parlor. The
second Daddy saw me, he started shaking his
head. "Uh-uh-uh" was all he said, but I got the
meaning full on.*

*"Here, honey, sit with me on the sofa," Mama
said as she squeezed me to her. "Look at you.
You're whiter than a ghost."*

*I didn't tell Mama, but I wished she wouldn't
say the word "ghost" ever again.*

*"Well, don't go babying her, Rose," said Daddy.
"She's plenty old enough to know the dark can't
hurt her. Plenty old enough."*

Mama patted my arm and gave Daddy a harsh look. "Just so you know, Will, I don't care for the dark either."

Daddy just shook his head. "Uh-uh-uh."

I laid my head in Mama's lap. Before I closed my eyes, I spotted Daddy eyeing me. He was still shaking his head.

Well, truth be told, I'm afraid again. I'm afraid my whole life is about to go dark. I'm afraid of losing Mama, afraid of Erin's plan for revenge, and afraid if I back down to Erin, I'll only disappoint Daddy yet again. Yep, I'm scared. Only this time, I will not let it show.

I put the journal back into my drawer, on top this time, took a deep breath, and began to dress for school. Once I was ready, and had fully forced my fear deep down inside me, I went into Mama's room to wake her.

I stood there watching her sleep, pretending she was her old self again—loving and happy, with a twinkle in her eyes. Each morning when I went to wake her, I said a little prayer that when she opened her eyes, the twinkle would be there once again, replacing the blank stare that had slowly grown worse over the past weeks.

I shook her gently. "Good morning, Mama. Time to get up."

She rolled over to look at me. No twinkle.

I pulled back the covers and helped her to her feet.

She sat slumped over on the edge of the bed while I took out her clothes for the day—her pink floral dress with the lace collar and white buttons. It was a little too fancy for wearing around the house, but Mama wouldn't protest, and I liked the way the pink brightened her face.

Mama slowly put the dress on and I helped her with the buttons. She should've worn silk stockings, but I never made her. I thought they'd feel itchy and uncomfortable, and she wasn't going out anyway.

I gently wiped her face with a damp washcloth and sat her down in front of her dresser. Her hair fell loose and wavy down her back. I took her brush and smoothed it. It was soft and thick and dark as molasses. Silvery hairs were beginning to appear in front. I brushed it back and braided it neatly. Mama would've preferred a bun, but I liked the braid. It made her look younger. A bun was the expected way for Mama to wear her hair, and most days, I did as I should. But about once a week, I did it my way—braid.

Standing back, I admired my handiwork. She looked beautiful in her pink dress with her braided hair.

I reached for her arm. "Outside today, Mama?"

She nodded ever so slightly. I took her book from the bedside table and walked her to the back porch. On rainy or stormy days, I had her sit in the parlor, but on nice days, I let her sit on the back porch.

Mama once told me that our house had no back porch when she and Daddy first moved in, not long before I was born. Daddy added it so Mama could sit outside in the fresh air with her knitting or sewing while he fished down at the pond or worked out in the field. He even made it covered so she wouldn't get burned in the sun or wet in the rain. Once I was old enough to fish with Daddy, Mama would sit in her rocker and watch us any time she wasn't too busy fixing supper or straightening the house or scrubbing the laundry. We'd wave and she'd wave back. Sometimes I'd hold up a big fish for her to see. She'd clap and call out, "That's a fine one, honey. Real fine."

On the day Daddy left, it was like an invisible rope got tied around Mama and pulled her out to the porch. It kept on pulling her out there every day after. I figured it made her feel closer to Daddy.

Once she was comfortable in her rocker and clutching her book, I went into the kitchen to make her some coffee. I'd left a few biscuits in the cookstove warmer the night before, so I didn't bother making anything else. Wasn't much else anyhow. Gone were the days when Mama made hot biscuits smothered in sausage gravy, or crisp bacon or smoked ham to go with our eggs. Not that we needed it. It didn't take much to fill me, and Mama had started eating like a sick bird.

I took her skimpy breakfast onto the porch and sat it on the wooden table beside her. Kneeling in front of her, I gently eased the book from her hands. "Here. I'll read to you while you eat."

This was our morning routine. I read to her. She ate. I hoped the proverbs comforted her in some way. Back

41

when Mama had packed my lunch, she'd put in a note with a proverb on it. It was like getting a little present every day. Sometimes I understood them, most times I didn't, but I missed seeing them now. I flipped through the dog-eared pages of her book to the place I'd left off—page 154.

"'Graceful Proverbs.'" I looked up at Mama to see if she was listening. She was taking tiny sips of her coffee and seemed to be concentrating. I prayed it was on me. "'A closed fist is the lock of heaven and the open hand is the key of mercy. A gem is not polished without rubbing, nor a man perfected without trials.'" I paused at that. I hoped God was perfecting us good if that one was true, 'cause trials were exactly what we were going through.

I read on for a little while, long enough for Mama to finish her coffee and eat half her biscuit. Once it sat on the plate for longer than a couple minutes, I knew she was done with it. I ended my reading with: "'A widow is a rudderless boat.'" Now, I know Mama likes her proverbs, but that one sounded downright rude to me.

I returned Mama's book to her and we sat there for a while in silence, watching the pond ripple in the breeze and listening to the finches and sparrows chattering in the trees. The crisp morning air cooled my skin, and I breathed in the scents it carried—the sweetness of Mama's roses, the warm grassiness of the field, and the soapy smell of Mama herself. The familiar scents and Mama's touch soothed me, and for a moment all the uncertainties of my new life—life without Daddy—faded.

"When will your father be home?" Mama murmured after a while. It was the question she'd asked each morning since Daddy had left.

I'd become used to my reply. "I'm not sure, Mama. You know how he is. He never comes home till his work's done."

Usually Mama would sigh and grin slightly, forming something close to a smile, but not this time. I didn't understand. It'd been the right answer every other day. Why wasn't it now? I wondered if she was giving up on Daddy, and I knew I couldn't let her. If Mama gave up on him, did that mean I should too?

Mama looked up at me—not around me or through me, but at me. Behind her darkened eyes I could see the faintest twinkle of life. She reached over and stroked my hair. "Down for hair, just like your father."

I thought of Erin and her threat, and for one second, I truly believed Mama was getting better and everything would be all right. Then the second ticked past, and Mama's eyes went blank once again, staring out across the field, out across time. But she had come back. I knew she had more surely than I'd ever known anything. Maybe I could bring her back again. I had to try.

"I've got school today, Mama. Can I get you anything before I go?"

How could I have known I'd said the wrong word—one tiny word that would push her further away from me? I hadn't known, and I held my breath, afraid to blink, waiting for a reply that didn't come.

~ Six ~

When I Did Well, I Heard It Never;
When I Did Ill, I Heard It Ever

The first week of May flew by. And yet it dragged. The time I spent fishing with Ben melted away faster than butter in the hot sun, but the time I spent at school passed as slowly as ice melting in the icebox. Still, I was glad for it to be May. My birthday was at the tail end of it, and I couldn't help but think maybe Daddy would show up on that very day. He'd be the best birthday present. Surely he knew that.

Erin spent all week nagging me at recess and whispering warnings into my ear during class. She insisted I take my name off the contest list or else. I figured by the time Friday rolled around I'd be glad to see it, but I wasn't. This Friday wasn't gonna be a good one. I could feel it in my bones. And when Ben didn't show up to walk with me to school, I almost marched myself right back home. Almost.

Miss Jones strode up and down the aisles of desks, passing out graded math tests. Each step she took echoed through the room. I gasped for air. A big butterfly had set up house inside my stomach, and its fluttering was making it hard to breathe. More than anything, I wanted to hear "my own Lizzie Girl" when Daddy came home, and bad grades would kill my chances. Hard as I'd try to hide them from him, he had his ways of finding out.

The echoes grew louder as Miss Jones came closer. The butterfly whooped and whooshed around inside me, and I thought I might be sick. I squeezed my eyes shut, picturing a perfect A written at the top of my test. I figured if I pictured it hard enough it might really be there.

"Excellent work, Erin," Miss Jones whispered behind me.

Great. An A for Erin. Paper shuffled beside me. I squeezed my eyes tighter. A wisp of air blew against my face as Miss Jones placed my test in front of me. I kissed my locket for luck, then looked. D!

"Lizzie, I'd like to see you after school, please."

Boiling blood rushed through my body, but chill bumps covered my arms. My stomach felt full and heavy, like I'd swallowed one of the boulders outside the school. Never in my entire life had I gotten a D, but there it was, staining the page in red pencil. Pencil so red it screamed at me. D wasn't much better than F, and F meant failure. Is that what I was? I couldn't sleep if I tried; I hadn't caught

One-Eye; and now this. I was a failure. A failure without Daddy. And as soon as he got back, he was gonna figure that out.

Behind me, Erin stifled a laugh. I flipped the test over, but I knew she'd seen. The D was so big you could've seen it from outside. Maybe from across town! Her seat popped as she sat back. I imagined her sitting there, arms crossed, eyes glowing with satisfaction. Lucky for her we were in school; otherwise I'd have knocked that look right off her face.

I tried to read Miss Jones's expression as I approached her desk after school. Her lips were turned upward in a slight smile, but her thick brows were rumpled with worry.

"You wanted to see me, Miss Jones?"

"Yes, I want to make sure you're all right." Her tone was gentle but firm. "I've been worried about you since your father left. Your grades are dropping—first the B on your spelling test several weeks ago, and now this. You haven't made less than an A in ages. You're distracted. I can see it in class. You know if you need to talk to me, I'm here. Is something bothering you?" Miss Jones could spot liars with her eyes shut, but I had to try. I couldn't tell her how worried I was about Mama, or how I had to spend most of my time on things like laundry and cooking. First, she might call Dr. Heimler. No way could I let that happen. Second, she might think I shouldn't be home alone with Mama. Then what? They'd take me away from her. I couldn't chance it.

"No, ma'am," I said. My palms began to sweat, just as they always did when I was in trouble with Daddy. I clasped them behind my back to keep her from seeing their slimy wetness. "I've just been busy, that's all."

Miss Jones sat in front of me, her brows nearly touching. She chewed her bottom lip for a moment, then spoke. "Busy doing what? I can't stand by and watch my best student falter. School's nearly out for the year, and you don't want to start ruining your hard work now. I stay after school a few afternoons a week and help some of the other students. Would you like to join us?"

Extra help? I didn't have time. I had to get home as quick as I could each day after school to check on Mama. I crossed my fingers behind my back. "No, thank you. I'll be fine."

Her chair grated the floor as she stood. "Well, I think I'll stop by and have a chat with your mother. Something needs addressing."

"No, Miss Jones!" I blurted. Visions of Miss Jones attempting to have a talk with Mama sent the butterfly into a complete frenzy. "I promise. Everything's fine. The D was my fault. I was fishing with Ben when I should've been studying. Please don't speak to Mama. It won't happen again."

She opened her mouth to reply, but the door flew

open and slammed against the wall. A loud bang echoed through the room.

"She's lying, Miss Jones!" I should've known. A snooping Erin barged in to have her say.

"Young lady, what do you mean, interrupting us like this?"

"I'm interrupting to tell you Lizzie's lying. Flat out to your face. Her grades aren't dropping because of Ben Butler, they're dropping because her daddy deserted her, her mama is too sick to even come out, and it's too much for her to handle. She doesn't belong in school, she belongs in an orphanage. Because an orphan is exactly what she is."

"I am not an orphan! Don't you dare call me that." I started to head over and knock Erin straight off her high horse, but her eyes lit up as I moved toward her. I stopped. That was exactly what she wanted. She was trying to rile me up so I'd smack her, the same way I'd smacked Scott McClain. Well, for once she wasn't gonna get her way.

Erin shrank away from me, even though I hadn't come one inch closer. "Help, Miss Jones! She's gonna hit me!" she squealed.

Miss Jones looked at me to check that I wasn't. I shrugged. "Don't be ridiculous, Erin. Lizzie's standing perfectly still. And I will not have name calling, do you understand? Furthermore, there is no reason to believe that Mr. Hawkins deserted his family, and until Dr. Heimler says Mrs. Hawkins is too sick to care for Lizzie,

I'll simply not listen to any more. I'm sure Mrs. Hawkins has her hands full at home with Mr. Hawkins gone."

Most students don't like their teachers very much, if for no other reason than they're the ones who make us use our brains, but at that moment Miss Jones was my favorite person in the world. She wanted proof, and Erin couldn't get it. Nobody could prove Daddy'd gone hobo any more than I could prove he hadn't. And as for Dr. Heimler examining Mama, well, I'd be able to kiss my elbow before I'd let that happen.

"But—" Erin began.

"You two girls are going to have to get over this little rift you've started with each other," Miss Jones interrupted. "I won't have it in this school. Both of you apologize this minute."

It's funny how you can love somebody one minute and despise them the next, but that is exactly how my opinion of Miss Jones changed.

Erin stared at me. I stared right back.

"Well?" said Erin. "I'm waiting."

It was time to see who was gonna apologize first, and it wasn't gonna be me. "You'll have to keep waiting, because I am not apologizing to you."

Erin's nostrils flared like she was a bull about to charge. "Don't think I'm apologizing to you, either. I've had it with you and your Miss Perfect ways. You're not any better than me. If Miss Jones wants proof your mama is crazy, she's gonna get it!"

"Girls!" Miss Jones shouted above Erin. "That's enough! If you two don't apologize immediately, both of you are out of the essay contest next week. I will not reward this type of behavior with extra credit."

The thought of giving Erin the satisfaction of hearing me say "sorry" made that boulder in my stomach lurch. Miss Jones probably thought at least one of us would choose the extra credit. She could think that till the cows came home, but I'd take another D before I'd tell Erin Sawyer I was sorry when I absolutely was not.

"Miss Jones, you may take me out of the contest." I walked over to the blackboard and erased my name from the list. "I don't need it."

Miss Jones sighed. "Not the choice I'd hoped for, but . . . Erin?"

Erin gulped a breath of air. She turned and faced the list of names. "Erin Sawyer" remained on the board in her curlicue cursive just under the chalk smudge that had been my name. Her pinched-up face relaxed, softening her scowl to a semismile. She sashayed over to me. "I'm sorry, Lizzie. I shouldn't have said those things about your family. Will you forgive me?" She put out her hand like I'd actually take it.

The room started to spin. Faster and faster. My fingernails dug into my palms. "You don't mean that, Erin Sawyer!" I yelled. "No, I most certainly do *not* forgive you."

"Lizzie!" Miss Jones grabbed my arm. "Thank you, Erin. I'll expect your essay next week. You may go."

Erin sauntered out the door, but now I knew better than to believe she'd really gone. Miss Jones turned to me and placed her hands on my shoulders. She studied me hard, as though she was trying to see straight into my soul. "I expected better of you, Lizzie. You'd best patch things up with Erin. Life's too short to be holding grudges. They only cause more trouble than they're worth."

"Yes, ma'am."

She looked at me for a second longer before turning to her desk. She slid an envelope off its slick wooden surface and handed it to me. "Now." She exhaled hard, like she was breathing out all that had just happened. "Would you be so kind as to run Ben's paper and today's assignments over to him on your way home? Tell him we missed him today, and I hope he is well."

"Yes, ma'am."

She nodded my dismissal.

Outside, clouds had gathered, turning the sky a bluish gray. If my emotions had a color, that was it. The only person who could brighten me was Ben. I was glad to have an excuse to drop by and see him, but Mama needed me home, so I'd have to make it quick.

I hurried out of the schoolyard toward the road, but an unwelcome figure emerged from behind an oak to block my way.

"Looks like your name came off that list after all." Erin twisted her brown braids around her fingers. "Too bad you didn't apologize. Now you're stuck without extra credit."

"At least I didn't lie. You didn't mean what you said to me, and I sure as heck wouldn't have meant any apology I'd have given you."

"Well, Miss Jones told us we had to apologize. She didn't say we had to mean it."

I shoved past her, hoping I might knock her down. I didn't, and her mouth kept right on running. "You're about to get what you deserve, and I'll be the one to give it to you. You think you're so much better than me with all your As, and your I'm-not-scared-of-you ways, and always having Ben by your side. Well, you're not. You can't go around showing off all the time and not pay a price. For once, I'm going to beat you."

"I do not go around showing off. Sounds to me like you're jealous."

"Of what? Once my mama tells Dr. Heimler about your mama, you'll have nothing but yourself."

I whirled around to face her. "Tell him what about my mama? You don't know a thing about her. You just like to think you do."

"Oh, yes, I do. I know for a fact she's gone loopy, and once Dr. Heimler ships her off to the hospital, the sheriff'll be shipping you off to the orphanage. Then you'll be out of my hair for good." Erin's lips curled upward in an all-too-knowing grin. "You can lie to Miss Jones all you want, but I know the truth about you. I've got my ways of knowing. Ways you'd never even think of."

I didn't say anything back. There wasn't any point. She wasn't gonna hush even if I wired her mouth shut. Besides, now I had a new problem to think about. A big one. I had to make sure Dr. Heimler was kept as far away from Mama as possible. One look at her and he'd deliver her straight to the hospital and I'd never get her back. The thought of her left in there alone sent shivers shooting down my spine. And if either Erin or Dr. Heimler thought I was gonna let her go, they could kiss my grits.

Beside me, Erin matched my stride step for step, but she kept quiet. I guess she figured her presence alone was enough to make me sick, and she was right.

At the fork in the road I went left and she went right. Now I didn't have to guess. I knew exactly where she was headed—to blab to her mother about mine.

Seven

Life Is Like the Moon: Now Full, Now Dark

The sky was steadily darkening, so I sped up. I couldn't go home until I'd given Ben his papers, and I wanted to tell him about Erin. Besides Mama, Ben was the best listener in the world. I'd tried talking to Daddy a time or two, but I'd been badgered in return. I hated badgering—being told the bad in my life was my own fault and that I needed to buck up and do something about it. Ben never badgered. He'd listen and nod and agree. He'd let me spill out all the ugly I wanted. I loved him for it.

I entered Ben's yard and the butterfly that'd plagued me all day died. The Butlers' place was like a warm quilt to me, comforting and cozy. Two years back, I'd helped them paint the house a fresh coat of sunny yellow. Now the house seemed to smile at me each time I came to visit. Mrs. Butler's six Rhode Island Reds welcomed me, clucking and pecking their way across the front yard. They were allowed free range as long as they kept away from the white azaleas planted in front of the porch. The azaleas had shed most of their blooms. I was reaching for one when Mrs. Butler came around from the back of the house.

"Oh, Lizzie, it's you. I thought I heard someone."

Dirt smudged her face and covered her hands. She always did her gardening at this time of day, and today was no exception. She was a woman with a strict schedule and a particular way of doing things, and you could bet your last penny she'd never change any of it. The slightest variation threw her into a loop for days. She'd been like that since I could remember, but she'd gotten worse when Mr. Butler died.

"Hi, Mrs. Butler," I said. "Is Ben home?"

She scrubbed her hands on her apron and smiled. "Be just a minute, dear. Would you like something to drink?"

"No, thank you," I said. "I need to make it quick."

She nodded and disappeared into the house.

A few minutes later, Ben emerged. He plopped down onto the bottom step of the porch. "Looks like rain," he muttered, though he was studying his slingshot, not the sky.

I handed him the envelope. "Miss Jones asked me to bring this by. How'd you do?"

He tore it open and unfolded the papers. He held up his test, revealing a big fat B. "Good enough for me."

I shoved my test under his nose. I stood there waiting for the shock of it all to sink in, but he only shrugged and pushed the sheet away. "What happened?" he asked. He might as well have been asking what happened while I was washing dishes or hanging clothes on the line.

"Well, you know how busy I've been at home. I thought I could pull at least a B. Guess not."

Ben picked up a fistful of dirt and let it sift through his fingers. "I reckon you'll live. There are worse things in the world than a bad grade."

"Yeah, like my worst enemy having the satisfaction of seeing it."

I could see Ben watching me out of the corner of his eye. A new fistful of dirt drifted to the ground.

"Just go on and say it," I said.

Ben heaved a breath. "I think you should do what Erin wants. What does one stupid contest matter anyhow?"

"It doesn't matter anymore. Me and Erin got into it after school, and Miss Jones told us to apologize or else we'd be out of the essay contest. I wasn't about to say I was sorry. But Erin did just so Miss Jones would let her stay in. Made me so mad I could've spit."

"Awww, Lizzie!" Ben threw a rock into the yard. "You should've just went on and done it. Erin did. What's the big deal? Ain't you got bigger problems than beating her?"

An invisible fist punched me in the stomach. "Me beating her? I think you got that backwards, 'cause it's always her trying to beat me."

Ben didn't reply. He jumped up from the steps and snatched up another rock. He put it in the sling and shot it into the air. The snap of the rubber made something snap inside me. I grabbed the slingshot from him and jabbed it into his stomach. "Would you listen to me and stop with the slingshot already? If I knew how to work this thing, I'd pop a rock right between your eyes!"

Ben jerked the slingshot away and shoved it into his back pocket. "Then it's a good thing I never showed ya how. You know, if you weren't so worried about your own troubles, maybe you'd have time to think about somebody else's."

"Are you calling me selfish? Because it seems to me I'm the one with the problems around here."

Ben looked at me, his cheeks flushed and his usually soft green eyes hardened to a steel gray. His jaw twitched. "Sure, you've got your problems," he yelled, "but maybe some of them are your own doing! Other folks got troubles they can't do nothin' about. Ain't you even gonna ask me why I wasn't at school today, or are you just too worried about *you* to care?"

That invisible fist kept right on punching. Harder and harder. Knocking the breath from me. Ben was badgering. The one person in the whole world I trusted to never do it *was* doing it. "Fine, then. Why weren't you at school today, Ben?"

"Because I started over at Mr. Reed's today helping him around his farm. Pays me three and a half dollars a week."

"What? You mean creepy ol' Mr. Reed just came up and asked you to work for him?"

"Course he didn't ask me. I went and asked him. You know the shape his place is in, and he ain't exactly a spring chicken. I figured he was my best shot, so I asked him. I can't just keep sittin' around here waitin' for the bank to take our house. School'll have to wait."

I looked at Ben, struggling to understand what he meant. "You're telling me you asked Mr. Reed for help?"

"Yeah, Lizzie, I reckon that's what I'm telling ya." His voice needled me. "I forgot you don't understand what asking for help is."

No, I didn't understand what asking for help was. Daddy always said if you needed something, you had to get it yourself or do without. You weren't supposed to go around begging off folks—much less old folks who don't like company. But I wasn't about to get into a tiff with Ben over it.

"You mean you're not coming back to school . . . ever?"

"Not this year. Have to wait and see about next. School's nearly out anyway. Helping Ma is more important right now. I'm all she's got." He leaned in close and lowered his voice. "Mrs. Martin's quilt money wasn't enough. Payin' the mortgage ain't gonna happen."

Low thunder rumbled in the distance. Words, thoughts, time disappeared. Ben's shoulders slumped like all the life in him was being sucked out. He kicked at a patch of weeds with the toe of his boot. "I reckon you'd best be headin' home. Gonna storm, and I got chores to do." He forced a smile, then plodded up the steps. I thought he'd turn and wave, but he didn't. The screen door slammed behind him with a bang.

A light drizzle had started to fall by the time I reached the end of the drive. On any other day the cold drops would've forced me to pick up my pace. But this wasn't any other day. No siree. This was a day of disappointment. A day I wanted it to rain—rain so hard and so fast it'd soak right through my hair, down through my scalp, and into my brain, where it'd wash away all my worries and fears. Then the only thing left to think about would be the rain itself. At least until I got home.

God must've been listening in on my thoughts, because pour it did. And think about rain is exactly what I was forced to do. Sloppy red mud splashed around me with each step. I wanted to run, but that only made the mud splatter up onto my socks and the hem of my dress. Let me tell you, there's a world of difference between trudging through thick, goopy mud after all the extra water has drained away and sloshing through it when it's still thin and watery. My socks were ruined.

Once I made it home, I stripped off my shoes and socks and left them on the front porch. There wasn't any sense in traipsing through the house tracking mud all over the floor. Inside, I grabbed a blanket from the linen closet and went straight out to Mama. The rain had come up faster and heavier than I'd thought, and though the porch cover would keep her dry, I didn't want her sitting outside in the damp. I wrapped the blanket around her and moved her into her wingback chair in the parlor. She snuggled into it, and I went to change out of my wet clothes.

My well-worn overalls soothed me after my fuss with Ben. They felt like fishing and bare feet and good times. Somehow they made me feel that everything would be all right between Ben and me, even if I didn't know how to get "all right" back.

Over a bowl of dumplings and a square of dry corn bread, I read to Mama from her book. I needed it to comfort me as much as I hoped it comforted her. "Graceful Proverbs" continued: "A woman without religion, a flower without perfume. A man without religion is like a horse without its bridle. Broad is the shadow of generosity."

I read to her for over an hour, finally stopping at "Impossibilities and Absurdities in Proverbs." I placed the book back in Mama's lap and went to clean the kitchen and put the leftover corn bread in the cookstove warmer. It'd taste good later, crumbled into some milk.

After I'd helped Mama into her nightgown and put her to bed, I was more than ready to fall into my own bed. The day had worn on me. I didn't know what to do about Erin—or Ben. My eyes watered and burned, needing to close, needing to rest. But, same as every other night, sleep ran from me.

I pulled my journal from the drawer, closed my eyes, and counted four pages in. I opened my eyes and began to write.

I've been close with Ben for a long time now. I don't want to think about what it'd be like without him. But it seems like here lately, I just can't figure him out. He wants me to go on and give Erin her way. Lose to her. Take a hit on my grades to make her feel better. That doesn't seem fair, and that's not what Daddy would want. The last time I gave up my grades for somebody—for Ben—it only got me into trouble.

February was terribly cold last year. Ben's father came down with influenza and was bedridden for close to two weeks before he passed. Dr. Heimler tried everything he knew, and Ben refused to leave his pa's side the whole time. Mrs. Butler and me watched Ben helping Dr. Heimler.

"You just watch, Lizzie," she said. "My boy's gonna be a doctor someday."

Everybody nursed and prayed, and nursed and prayed some more, but I guess God decided He needed Mr. Butler more than Ben and his ma did.

I've never seen Ben so quiet. He mostly just sat and fiddled with his slingshot, tugging at its rubber band. Mrs. Butler even let him carry it to the funeral home.

He did good at the funeral, standing straight and tall, shaking everybody's hand and thanking them for coming. I was standing there with him, both of us watching Mama comfort Mrs. Butler, when I spotted a thin, shadowy figure standing alone at the very back of the dark room. I pointed the figure out to Ben. Ben didn't blink an eye. He walked right up to the man and put out his hand. "Thank you for coming, Mr. Reed." Mr. Reed reached out and took Ben's hand. He nodded once. Then he was gone.

I about fainted clean away. I'd hardly ever seen Mr. Reed in town, much less at anybody's funeral. But there he was. And there he'd gone.

Ben stayed home for a few days after the funeral, and I went straight to his house each day after school. I'd stay with him till long after suppertime. Mama didn't seem to mind, but Daddy did.

"Lizzie Hawkins," he said. "Don't you have a spelling bee coming up the first week of March?"

"Yes, sir. The first Friday."

"Well, then, you'd best get to studying. I'm telling you, you're gonna be something one day—something better than all of us. You understand? God don't waste miracles, and you're a miracle. He meant you for something great, otherwise why were you born at all? And let me tell you, young lady, that path to greatness starts at school. I want top grades, and I don't expect anything less. Neither does He."

"Yes, sir. I can do it."

And I could've, but I didn't. I couldn't stand the thought of Ben being without me. When the spelling bee rolled around, I placed fourth out of twelve kids. Mama clapped and smiled but Daddy looked at me like I'd just crushed his heart to smithereens. I struggled to hold back the tears. Tears would only make him madder.

"I thought you were listening when I told you I expected first place. You've got God-given brains, Elizabeth, and you're gonna use 'em."

"Yes, sir."

"I know what happened. You were too busy playing around with Ben Butler to study, and I'm not having that again. You're forbidden to go over to Ben's or to have him over here for two weeks, and I don't want to hear any lip about it either."

"Yes, sir."

"Now you go to your room and consider what you've done. Mama will call you when it's time for supper."

When Mama came in a little over an hour later, she tried her best to smooth things over. "Don't fret about it, honey. Daddy's just got a lot on his mind right now, that's all. He wants you to do your best so maybe someday you won't have to struggle through things the way we are now.

Understand? He's only hard on you because he loves you."

I leaned into Mama. She wrapped her arms around me and my tears flowed freely.

"You've been good to Ben, Lizzie, and I know Daddy might not agree, but I think that's more important than any spelling bee. There'll be other bees, and I'm sure you'll do better next time. Remember, failure is not falling down, but refusing to get up. You'll get back up. You were born to. That's something your father and I do agree on."

I squeezed Mama tight before I let her go. A tear spot marred the front of her dress. She took her handkerchief and dabbed it. "I know you wouldn't want Daddy to see. Now, get washed up and come to supper. You'll feel better after you eat."

After Mama left, I made a secret promise to myself. I would get back up, just like she said, but never ever again would I let myself fall.

So what am I supposed to do now? Do I fall on purpose to make Ben and Erin happy? Or do I keep fighting to be the best I can be, no matter who it hurts?

~ *Eight* ~

If Not for Hope, the Heart Would Break

I realized real quick that Saturdays weren't gonna be worth a drop in the bucket without Ben around. Watching Mama rocking back and forth was taking its toll. I wanted to help her, but I didn't know how. I had to get out of the house, but I refused to leave till late afternoon. Everybody in Bittersweet, me included, knew Dr. Heimler's rounds ran like clockwork on Saturdays. He started at nine in the morning and was done by four. But if Mrs. Sawyer had believed Erin, and she probably had, he'd be stopping by sooner rather than later. I didn't want to chance him showing up with me gone.

The best thing to do in the meantime was to get to the massive pile of dirty clothes. As long as I could remember, Monday had been wash day, but now that I was in charge of the washing, it had to be Saturday or Sunday because of school. And today was just as good as tomorrow.

First thing was to set the water in the big iron pot

behind the house to boiling. It had filled with rainwater, so I started a fire under it and shaved in most of my last cake of lye soap. By the time I'd hauled out the rubboard, three tin tubs (one for the soapy water, the other two for rinsing), and stripped the sheets from our beds, steam was beginning to curl from the pot.

I got busy separating the clothes and linens into not-so-dirty and way-too-dirty piles—the dirtiest would be the last to get scrubbed. They always turned the water murky. I was lucky. The way-too-dirty pile had just one article in it: the dress I'd been wearing when Erin pushed me into the mud. Even after all the fishing I'd done, my overalls went into the not-so-dirty pile. And, of course, anything Mama had worn didn't have a speck of dirt on it.

With the rest of my lye in hand, I soaped and scrubbed each article, rubbing the stained parts hard over the rub-board. The tops of my arms shook like jelly with each pass up and down the board, but I liked it. When you're concentrating on scrubbing the stain out of a dress, you don't have room to be thinking about anything else. You just keep saying to yourself: *Rub. Scrub. Stain going. Rub. Scrub. Stain gone.*

Once the stains were gone (or mostly gone, in the case of my school dress), I tossed all the whites, like sheets and underthings, into the boil pot. While the whites were boiling, I rinsed out the colored things in the tubs holding clean water and wrung them out. Then, with a big wooden scooper, I fished out the whites from their boiling bath. The rinse water wasn't so clear by the time I got through with it. It got dumped.

I hung all the wash out on the clothesline to dry and doused the fire under the big iron pot. Once the water had cooled to warm, I made good use of it by hauling buckets of it to the front porch and scrubbing down the wood.

I stood back and admired my handiwork. Clean sheets billowed in the breeze and the porch was free of unsightly mud marks. I figured I'd pretty well earned my late-afternoon break. And I knew just where I'd take it: Hinkle's General Store. One thing I could be sure of when it came to Hinkle's is that they would never, ever be out of Goo Goo Clusters. Eating one would cost me something, but smelling them was free. Besides, now that I'd used my last cake of lye, I needed to head down there and make a trade anyway.

I moved Mama inside to her chair in case Dr. Heimler decided to drop by this late. I fixed her a piece of dry toast and a cup of coffee, then went into the garden to gather some fresh broccoli, onions, and peas to bring to Hinkle's. I'd been raised to keep my hands off the emergency savings jar Mama and Daddy had always kept behind the plates in the kitchen cabinet, except in a true emergency. I didn't think I had a true emergency yet. I'd been feeding me and Mama just fine by fixing vegetables from our garden and catching fish from the pond. I traded any extras for other things I needed from Hinkle's.

I could hear Ziggy in a barking ruckus all the way from the town welcome sign. The sign read: WELCOME TO

67

BITTERSWEET, A GREAT PLACE TO GROW. FOUNDED 1843. Bittersweet residents prided themselves on keeping the sign in like-new condition. The red, green, and yellow paint looked freshly painted. Though why our town was called Bittersweet, I'd never understood. Wasn't any around.

I rubbed the sign as I passed. It looked smooth as silk from afar, but it was rough as a corncob to the touch. A splinter stuck into my finger. By the time I worked it out, I was rounding the bend onto Main Street. Ziggy was still in an uproar. I squinted up at Mr. Reed's, trying to catch a glimpse of Ben hard at work.

Not even going without Goo Goo Clusters could top the horridness of working for Mr. Reed. Three and a half dollars a week was good wages, but that didn't seem a fair amount when Mr. Reed was involved. He would've had to come up with seven or eight dollars before I'd go rambling around all the sun-baked squirrel tails and coon furs hanging off his house. Heck, just making it to the front door was worth at least a dollar. The only clean spot on the place was Ziggy's pen.

Mr. Reed took better care of that dog than most people take of their own children. I'd only been inside Mr. Reed's a few times, each time being with Daddy in the fall when he delivered a load of sorghum cane to Mr. Reed for milling. Walking into Mr. Reed's house was like walking into a cave. Dark and cold and dreary. Mr. Reed's meetings with Daddy were always short, but it was enough time for me to notice Ziggy's shiny silver bowl on the dirty kitchen floor and Mr. Reed's chipped ceramic one on the crumb-covered table. Mr. Reed had always been a few loops shy of a knot, but to me, this slapped a "crazy" stamp right between his eyes.

Though I knew Ben was somewhere among the mess, I couldn't spot him. And I wasn't about to go up there and track him down. Besides, he was probably still mad at me, and I'd promised myself I'd never again be around Ben when he was mad. It made me have a funny feeling, like I was suffocating on air. I headed on into Hinkle's.

The bell above the door clanged as I entered. Brightly colored cans and boxes filled every spare space in the store, and tempting scents filled the air: freshly ground coffee beans, sweet peppermint, and vanilla. Mrs. Hinkle peered out from the back. "Lizzie Hawkins!" her shrill voice greeted me. "Wipe your feet before you come across this floor. I just swept it clean."

"Yes, ma'am." I wiped my feet, careful to remove every last speck of dirt. If I didn't, Mrs. Hinkle would have me sweep over the whole thing again, and I was sick of cleaning today.

She continued to eye me as I made my way over to the counter, her body not much taller, but far wider, than the broom handle she was grasping. Mrs. Hinkle has always been stern and scary; her black hair was slicked back into as tight a bun as possible, pulling the skin on her face too tight. I'd mentioned once to Daddy that I didn't like her. Daddy only nodded. He didn't like her either.

"Don't let her get to you, Miss Lizzie. The missus is just flustered because I'm making her take a trip with me into Birmingham. We're heading to the mission to help serve." Mr. Hinkle leaned forward on the counter, ducking out of his wife's view. His eyes twinkled. "She didn't take too kindly to that."

I giggled. Now, Mr. Hinkle I'd always liked. He was the closest I'd ever come to meeting Santa Claus—well, a skinny Santa. His cheeks were overly red and his eyes crinkled up at the corners like he was planning some way to break the rules—one of Mrs. Hinkle's rules.

I handed the vegetables to Mr. Hinkle. He looked through the sack and nodded. "Why, those are some of the prettiest heads of broccoli I ever did see. I do believe your mama is the best gardener in Bittersweet. Sure wish I was." He placed his hand over his heart and sighed. "Sadly, it wasn't meant to be."

"Mr. Hinkle, you're silly." Mr. Hinkle would never guess, but it wasn't Mama's skill that'd kept the garden going over the past month. It was mine.

"Don't I know it?" he said. "Now, back to business. I believe these are worth about seventy-five cents. Fair enough?"

"Yes, sir. I'll just take a trade this time." I handed him a list of the things I needed: more lye soap, some cornmeal, one pound of coffee for Mama, and one cake of Lifebuoy soap for bathing.

Mr. Hinkle nodded and I watched as he went around

gathering up my necessities. He brought my items over to the counter to sack them up for me.

"We'll be leaving for the mission just as soon as Mrs. Hinkle gets finished up and I close out the drawer. Hang around if you want to go."

"Sure would like to," I said, taking my bagged goods from him, "but I should probably be heading back home. Is it all right if I just look at the candy first?"

"Be my guest."

I'd asked Mr. Hinkle if I could look at the candy, but in truth, there was only one candy I cared about. Goo Goo Clusters. I hovered over the case, breathing in the air. It smelled sweet and chocolaty and peanutty. My mouth watered. I couldn't remember the last time I'd had one. The closest I could come to actually tasting their gooey goodness was taking deep sniffs of the brown paper bag in my bottom dresser drawer. But the scent had been near sniffed out. Only the faintest wisp of Goo Goo remained. The smell rising from the case was so fresh I could feel my teeth sinking into one. I closed my eyes and leaned forward. My locket tapped against the glass.

"What in heaven's name are you doing, child?" Mrs. Hinkle huffed as she scuttled past. "I swear, Herbert, I don't know what possesses young people today. Standing there drooling over candy. Can't they find some useful way to spend their time? You'd think she could at least pick up a broom or dustcloth instead of standing there idle."

I glanced over at Mr. Hinkle. He was shaking his head, not looking up from his figures.

"And what in heaven's name is that around your neck?"

I jerked up. Mrs. Hinkle was staring me down, one hand perched on her hip, the other gripping her trusty broom. "You didn't steal it, did you? Lord knows, and we well know, you can't afford a thing like that."

"No, ma'am, I did not steal it. My daddy gave it to me. It belonged to my grandmother."

Mrs. Hinkle perked up and edged closer. "You mean it's old? You know, they just don't make things the way they used to."

She was close enough now that I could see long black hairs poking from her nostrils. Why Mr. Hinkle had picked her to be his bride I'd never know. She reached out her fat fingers and wrapped them around my locket. I fought hard to keep from knocking them away.

"Herbert, why can't you ever find something like this for me? Your gifts are never right. Look and learn."

Mrs. Hinkle dropped the locket and shoved me toward Mr. Hinkle. He dutifully began to examine it. "Yes, dear, it's very nice."

"And it's been marked. That means nobody else in the world has one like it. Why in heaven's name a puny little girl has a thing like that and I don't is a mystery to me. Injustice. That's what it is."

Mr. Hinkle released the locket and I ran my fingers across its engraving, attempting to remove any last trace of Mrs. Hinkle. She turned and darted off into the back. I pictured her as a witch darting off on her broom, but the vision didn't work. She was too big. She'd have crashed that stick of a broom straight to the ground.

Mr. Hinkle stood scratching his chin, eyeing my locket. If he was thinking I was gonna give my locket to that witchy wife of his, he'd gone slap off his rocker. My hand balled around the only possession I had that proved I was meant to be more than a "puny little girl." I was meant for greatness. Daddy proved he still believed that when he left it for me. I'd worn it every day since he'd gone, and I refused to let it go now.

"You all right, Miss Lizzie?" Mr. Hinkle propped himself on his elbows, his eyebrows a furry mess of worry.

"Yes, sir. I'm fine." I gulped. "It's just that I know what you're thinking. And I'm sorry, but you can't have it. No one can."

He nodded. "So it's that important, huh? I could make you a real nice deal for keeping the missus off my back for a while. What do you say?"

My grip tightened around the locket and my mouth went as dry as cotton. "I can't," I said, looking Mr. Hinkle square in the eye. "Please understand."

I was beginning to think staying in the store to torture myself with the scent of Goo Goo Clusters had been a bad idea. Wasn't one of the Ten Commandments "Thou shalt not covet," or in Mama's words, "You can't always have what you want, so learn to want what you have"? Maybe God was punishing me for sinning.

Mr. Hinkle drummed his fingers on the counter, then reached over and patted my arm. "Your locket, your choice, Lizzie Hawkins." He winked and shuffled off into the back to find Mrs. Hinkle.

The tension eased, and a few minutes later I followed the Hinkles outside.

"You sure you won't go with us?" Mr. Hinkle asked as he opened the passenger door of his '29 Whippet for Mrs. Hinkle.

"I'm sure," I said. "Maybe next time."

"Sure thing. You have a nice evening, Miss Lizzie. I'll be seeing you around."

"Yes, sir." I waved them off and started back toward home, wishing the whole way that I could've gone with them. I hadn't taken a ride in a car since Daddy sold ours last year. The money he'd gotten for it had gone into the emergency savings jar in the kitchen cabinet. I'd seen him pull from that jar many times since. I couldn't help but wonder how much he'd taken from it on the morning he left. Now I was certain there wasn't much money left, and we had no car either.

That night, after I'd cleaned up dinner, read to Mama, and put her to bed, I took my journal from the drawer and opened it to a blank page. Seeing Mr. Hinkle drive away in that car had got me to remembering, and there was one memory in particular I wanted to stay in my journal forever.

In the summer of 1928, Daddy bought a used 1925 Ford Model T from Mr. Reeves, a man he worked with at the steel mill in Birmingham. I don't know how much Daddy gave for that car, but in my opinion it was worth whatever it took to buy it. I loved it. Daddy, Mama, and I took many drives in it, but it's the memory of that first drive that sticks out best.

It was a Sunday morning, our first trip to church in it. On the way, Mama sat up front with Daddy and I sat in the back alone. Daddy's thin frame bounced in unison with each bump in the road while his left arm crooked out the window, waiting to cast a friendly wave to passing neighbors. He smiled over at Mama, and she smiled right back. Then she turned to gaze out her window. Her mouth wasn't moving, but over the loud crunching of the tires on the dirt road I could hear her softly humming "Amazing Grace." A warm breeze blew in through the open window, bringing in the smells of fresh air and sun-baked dirt.

After church service, Mama decided she'd sit with me in the back to see what it was like. We bounced and jolted down the road, but pretty soon Mama went pale.

"What's the matter, Mama?" I asked her.

"I'm fine, honey," she whispered. "I'm just feeling a little sick."

"You want me to stop, Rose? I can pull over," Daddy offered from the driver's seat.

"No, I'll be fine."

But she wasn't fine. We didn't make it another half a mile before Mama started to gag. Daddy didn't waste any daylight pulling over. Mama stumbled out of the car and headed straight for the nearest bush. That was the most unladylike I've ever seen her, moaning and groaning, hunched over the bushes with her hands on her knees. Once she finished gagging, I offered to walk the rest of the way home with her. She accepted.

We had many Sunday drives after that, Daddy always crooking his arm out the window and Mama always humming "Amazing Grace" or "How Great Thou Art." When I die, I pray God lets Daddy drive me Home on a summer Sunday afternoon. But Mama will have to sit up front, no bones about it.

I closed my journal for the night and wondered if we'd ever be like that again—the three of us together and happy. I believed we would. I had to believe it. If my birthday wish came true, it'd happen sooner rather than later—on May 30.

I climbed into bed and kissed my locket. Though sleep didn't come easy, it did come—deep and dreamless.

~ *Nine* ~

Nice Doesn't Always Mean Good

My dreamless sleep lasted till around five-thirty. Better. I was taking it as a sign that maybe things in general were about to get better.

I'd barely finished cleaning up breakfast when there was a knock on the door. I knew by the knock exactly who it was. "Come on in, Ben," I called.

Ben tromped into the kitchen and plopped down at the table. My palms went cold and clammy at the thought of him still being mad at me. He looked all right, but looks could be deceiving.

He spoke first. "You wanna come down to Powell's with me? I figured you'd like to watch the buses."

The tone of his voice settled me. He sounded all right, too. "Sure," I said. "Just let me bring Mama in before we go."

I took his suggestion to watch the buses as a peace offering. Powell's Café was the local bus stop off the Bankhead Highway. It was fun to watch people as they got off the bus for a lunchtime rest on their way into Atlanta. You could see all kinds: men in business suits with matching hats; ladies with fancy purses and high heels; ill-behaved babies with tired mamas toting 'em around like potato sacks. It was strange to think of all these people, all from somewhere else, sitting there eating greens and butter beans right alongside the people I saw every day, right on a chair I'd most likely sat in myself. Course, Ben knew the *real* reason I liked to watch the buses these days, and it didn't have anything to do with interesting strangers. It had everything to do with Daddy.

I brought Mama inside, fixed her a glass of water, then took off with Ben. On the way, I told him all about Mrs. Hinkle wanting my locket and Mr. Hinkle aggravating her on purpose by making her serve soup at the mission. I tried to be funny in a few spots, but all I got from Ben was one measly chuckle.

Main Street was empty, not unusual for a Sunday morning. Everyone was too busy getting dressed for church to be out and about, but if you were still in town when church let out, the scene would change. Cars would zig and zag this way and that on their way home from church, and the non-churchgoers would crowd into Powell's around noon to get the Sunday special—a chicken dinner for thirty cents. I say non-churchgoers because all the saints in town went straight home after church for Sunday dinner with family—same as we had before Daddy left.

As it was, the only thing in the streets besides me and Ben was a blue Buick, and it appeared to be coming right at us. Only one man in town drove a car like that.

I felt Ben tap my arm, trying to get my attention. "Listen, Lizzie, I been needin' to talk to—"

I brushed his hand away and squinted at the car. "Is that who I think it is?" I watched as the car parked in front of us. Through the window I could make out a pale face with a thick mustache. I watched as lengthy limbs unfolded from the car. Yep. The very man I didn't want him to be. The last person in Alabama I wanted to run into besides Erin. He came toward us, his long legs taking even longer steps.

"Hey, Dr. Heimler," said Ben. "Headed to church?"

"Not this morning, I'm afraid. I'm on my way to the Martins'. One of their boarders is expecting and started having pains this morning. Still too early for that."

I tried not to look the doctor in the eyes. I prayed he hadn't pulled over for me. My prayer fell on deaf ears.

"This is my lucky day, Lizzie. You're just the person I needed to see. How's your mama?"

"Fine."

"Well, Mrs. Sawyer certainly seemed concerned about her this past Friday. She asked me to go see her, but I'm sorry to say I've had my hands full with patients. Some good help is what I need."

"Mama's all right. I think she's real tired, that's all."

Dr. Heimler stared at me with his near-black eyes.

"Well, sometimes fatigue can be a sign that something else is wrong. Why didn't you ask me to check on her?"

"I didn't want to trouble you," I lied, trying to say as little as possible, even though I'd already gone off and said too much.

"Well, just the same, I'll be by to see her. If there's something wrong, the longer she goes without a doctor, the worse she'll get."

"Yes, sir" was all I knew to say. I didn't want to get into an argument with Dr. Heimler over exactly what would happen to Mama if I let him look at her. I knew he'd just up and cart her off to the hospital whether I wanted him to or not.

We all stood in silence for a few seconds before Dr. Heimler broke it. "Well, I'd best be heading on. You let your mama know I'll be over to check on her by Friday. I mean it."

"Yes, sir," I said, though I didn't intend to let him set a toenail in our house.

Dr. Heimler tipped his hat. In less than a few seconds he was folded back into his car and driving down the street. When his car rounded the corner, I turned to Ben. He was shaking his head at me.

"What?" I asked.

"I don't know, Lizzie. Don't ya think maybe the doctor could help your mama? Maybe you should've told him the truth."

I stomped off toward Powell's. "No, I shouldn't have. You know what'd happen if I did."

Ben caught up to me. "What?"

"He'll put Mama in the hospital with all the crazies, and then what? She'll be alone, and I'll be sent away to the you-know-where."

"What if he can help without the hospital? I ain't never heard of Dr. Heimler sending somebody away like that."

I looked at Ben. I needed him to understand. "I can't chance it. Maybe he can help her, but what if he can't?"

Ben didn't reply; he just shook his head again. He thought I was wrong, but I knew I wasn't. We sat on the curb in front of Powell's Café and began tracing circles in the dirt with the toes of our shoes. Dust puffed into the air.

"And anyway," I said, trying one more time to convince him, "hasn't anybody ever told you that sometimes people aren't what they seem? If Daddy's told me that one time, he's told me a million."

"Well, I reckon he's right about that. There's lots of folks around here who ain't what they seem. Did ya know Mr. Reed was married once?"

Crabby old Mr. Reed married? Something about that picture didn't fit. "He couldn't have been. Who'd have married him?"

"I don't know who she was, but she was real pretty. I saw a picture of them together. It was sitting on a table in Mr. Reed's front room. He left me in there to go get my pay for the week. The man in the picture wasn't as skinny or wrinkled as Mr. Reed, but it was him—just a younger him."

"I wonder what happened to her."

"Well, when he came back he caught me staring at the picture, so I asked him about it. He picked it up and studied it. I'd swear I saw his chin quivering like he was about to cry, but maybe it was just his age. He kept on looking at the picture and told me that lady had been his wife. She died in childbirth not two years after they were married. The baby died less than a day later. Couldn't breathe right. He said he reckoned he hadn't talked about it to anybody in years. I asked him why he was all right with talkin' to me. Just like that, he stopped studyin' the picture and started studyin' me. He said he reckoned it was for two reasons: first, he knew I understood what it's like to lose someone you love, and second, I remind him of the little boy he might've had."

The gears in my brain were turning fast, trying to put everything Ben was telling me together. "Mr. Reed had a son?"

"'S what he said."

We sat for a while just thinking. Mr. Reed having a son once must've interested Ben for the thought of it to keep him quiet longer than five minutes. It interested me too. It was strange, and it proved the point I was trying to make about Dr. Heimler: people aren't always what they seem. Sometimes they seem worse than they are, sometimes better. But the trouble is you never can tell who is who. And that is why, as far as Dr. Heimler went, for Mama's sake, I'd have rather been safe than sorry.

~ *Ten* ~

A Loyal Heart May Be Landed
Under Traitor's Bridge

I held my breath all week long, waiting on a visit from the doctor. The way Erin flounced around me at school, you'd have thought he'd started on his way over five years ago. Of course, I guess her winning the sixth-grade extra credit on Wednesday gave her another reason to flounce. I let her believe she'd gotten the best of me for the time being. I thought it'd soothe her enough so she'd leave me alone for good.

When Saturday finally rolled around, with its cloudless sky and soothing warmth, Dr. Heimler still hadn't shown. I breathed a deep sigh of relief. I figured he'd been so busy he'd forgotten about Mama. I figured wrong.

I'd just finished hanging the last of the clean clothes out on the line when I spotted that all-too-familiar blue Buick coming up the drive. I grabbed the laundry basket and took off to the back porch to stand with Mama. I prayed he hadn't seen me take off across the yard. The roar of the car's engine grew louder as it approached the front of the house. Then came a shrill squeak from the brakes and the engine went silent.

For a moment, I could only hear the rhythmic rocking of Mama's chair and the rapid drumming of my own heart. In the quiet, both seemed louder than a marching band. One sound I could do nothing about, but the other I could. I gripped the back of Mama's rocker to stop its movement.

I pictured the doctor's long body leaving his Buick. The slam of a car door echoed through the air. Heavy footsteps tromped onto the front porch, sending vibrations through the house, right to the bottom of my feet. I held my breath, tightening my grip on Mama's rocker.

The world around me felt too still, too silent, as though the smallest of sounds would give me away. Of all the times for the birds to shut their beaks, why did it have to be now?

Five soft knocks floated through the air. They sounded far away and muffled, but they were close enough to make the baby hairs on my neck prick up.

I waited, afraid to move, listening for the sound of departing footsteps. Instead came five more muffled knocks. Mama must've heard too. She pulled against the grip I had on her chair.

"Mrs. Hawkins? Are you in there? It's Dr. Heimler."

Please, God, please. Just make him go away. Make him think we're not here. Still no footsteps.

Five more knocks, harder this time, pounded through the air. My fingers tingled, fighting to steady the chair.

Please. Make him go away. Make him leave. I released one hand long enough to grip my locket. I closed my eyes. *Please, please, please.*

Then, I heard them—the scuffle and stomp of departing footsteps, the roar of the car's engine, and the crunch of dirt and gravel beneath the tires. I let go of Mama and she started to rock—back and forth, back and forth, same as always.

I tiptoed through the house and peeped out the front window. Dr. Heimler's car was just turning out of our drive, a haze of dust boiling behind it.

I had no doubts. He'd be back, but it wouldn't be today. I had to get out of the house and into town. Fast. I wasn't supposed to be home, and though it sounded crazy, I'd have liked nothing better than to run right smack into the doctor. He'd see me in town and think I'd really been there the whole time. And if he asked about Mama, I'd tell him she was napping. Easy as pie.

I got myself ready and moved Mama inside. She resisted me at first, but she had to go in. Since Erin had threatened to have Mrs. Sawyer send Dr. Heimler, I hadn't left her outside alone. When I was in school, she was inside. When I was in town, she was inside. The only times Mama was able to enjoy her porch were those days I was home and able to keep an eye on the driveway. I was thankful she always stayed wherever I left her.

I made her comfortable in her chair, fixed her a glass of tea sweetened with a little sorghum syrup, double-checked she had hold of her book, then hurried into town. I was due to pick up some mending work from Mrs. Martin anyway. With all her boarders and housework, she didn't have the time for it. But I had studying time that'd changed over to working time, along with the lower grades to prove it.

I glanced up at Mr. Reed's when I passed. I hadn't talked to Ben in close to a week. I was beginning to think he'd rather be at Mr. Reed's than with me. Mr. Reed must've felt the same about Ben. The few times I'd been into town over the past week, I'd looked up and seen Ben hard at work hauling some of the larger pieces of junk out of Mr. Reed's yard. Working right alongside him was Mr. Reed himself. Even Ziggy was out of his pen, trailing Ben back and forth across the yard, his whole back end wagging. I didn't see any sign of life now, so I headed on to Mrs. Martin's.

I only squeezed in one and a half knocks before the door jerked open. Mrs. Martin shoved the bag of clothes into my hands so fast she pushed me backward. "Here you go, dear," she said, each word spoken faster than the last. "Need it back in a week. Let your mama know."

"Yes, ma'am. I'll te—"

I didn't even get "tell her" out before the door slammed shut again. I shrugged and started back home with my work. After Daddy lost his job, Mama did anything and everything she could to help bring in money—kept a garden with extra vegetables to trade, mended clothes, did laundry for elderly women. She'd taught me how to do those things too, so I could help her move through the work faster. More work getting done meant more money. I still kept up the garden and did some mending, but the laundry had had to go. It took me forever to do our own. Still, I'd learned from Mama pretty well. While I wasn't as skilled as her, I was good enough to keep Mrs. Martin believing Mama was the mender, not me.

I was just turning back onto Main Street when I spotted Ben coming out of Hinkle's. The sun beamed down like it was shining just on him. I threw up my hand and started to call out, but I changed my mind real fast when I saw who was coming out behind him: Erin. And she wasn't coming out at the same time by accident. She was coming out *with* him.

Her head whirled around in my direction. I ducked behind a parked car and watched them through the glass. She turned away and said something to Ben, then tilted her head back and laughed. I couldn't help but wonder if she was laughing at me.

The next few minutes felt like an eternity. Each second ticked painfully past as I watched my best friend, my only friend, laugh with the very person whose goal in life was to knock me down. Maybe that was it. Maybe the whole scene being played out in front of me was Erin pushing herself on Ben, trying to take away the last person on earth who cared about me. But Ben. Ben was letting her do it.

A spark of anger ignited within me and slowly, slowly, began to burn. I wanted to march right over to them and give Erin a piece of my mind, and then walk away from Ben, leaving him standing there feeling the same disappointed hurt I was feeling. But I didn't.

I watched Ben talk to Erin as though he didn't mind that she was the one person trying to destroy everything I cared about. A throbbing ache began to overpower the small flame of anger. The ache ran through my body, turning my feet to bricks—bricks too heavy for my legs. Bricks mortared to the ground.

They passed Powell's and rounded the corner, walking side by side. Even though they'd gone, I continued to watch the world through the glass. I couldn't move. I didn't want to. I grasped my locket and prayed that Ben was just being Ben—a peacemaker too nice to be mean, even to a girl like Erin. He'd always seen the good in people, even those with the darkest of hearts. Ben wouldn't betray me. Would he? What if he'd talked to her before? Many times before? Times I knew nothing about? I shuddered at the thought of it.

Ben had never once lied to me. My feet grew lighter, and I turned toward home. The small flame of anger flickered deep inside me, encased in a mountain of hurt. But the mountain had a crack in it, and through that crack emerged a sliver of hope. Ben would tell me the truth about him and Erin and, as sure as I was breathing, I was going to ask him to tell it.

Visions of Erin and Ben walking down the street flashed through my mind all evening—during supper, during my nightly reading to Mama, and after I'd readied Mama for bed. The visions still hadn't left me by the time I pulled my journal from my dresser drawer.

May 14, 1932

If I could ask God any question right now, it'd be: Why did You have to let Erin Sawyer come to Bittersweet? If I could ask God a second question, it'd be: Why did she have to hate me so much? I didn't even know she hated me that much till I scored the highest grades in class at the end of last term. She'd been here since August, and the only other time I'd seen her look so mad was when Myra "Rumor" Robinson spread the adopted secret.

"You're not gonna be the best for long, Hawkins, now that I'm here." Her voice had pounded me like a hammer on a nail. Determined. Forceful. But that was her voice. Her eyes told a different story. They were welling up with tears. "I'm better than you, and I'm gonna prove it."

"Well, don't go thinking I'm about to start losing to you, because I'm not."

And I wasn't. If she wanted to beat me, she'd just have to try harder.

"You'd better if you know what's good for you. Don't forget"—she leaned over into my space—"what happens to people when they mess with me. Myra was scared of dogs, and you're scared of something too. I'll find out what it is. I always find out."

"I'm not scared of you. Why do you care so much about winning anyway?"

Erin looked at me like I was three bricks shy of a load just for asking. "Why do you?"

The question pricked. I knew why I cared. I had to be the best because it was the only way I could be sure I was good enough in Daddy's eyes. I looked into Erin's unrelenting glare. I figured maybe she felt that way too. But we couldn't both be the best at everything.

Erin might've been mad about my grades, but Daddy was the proudest I'd seen him. He ran all around town telling anybody who'd listen that his Lizzie Girl was the smartest kid in sixth grade. It was the most I'd seen him smile since he'd lost his job.

When you get top honors in your grade, they put your name in the "School News" section of the Bittersweet Times, *and Daddy carried that paper around with him all through Christmas. I knew I'd* redeemed myself from my fourth-place finish in the spelling bee last March.

Mama was happy too. To celebrate, she baked my favorite dessert—yellow cake with chocolate icing. After I helped her clean the kitchen, we sat down in the parlor to mend a pair of pants and a few shirts. Daddy never sat with us when we did our work. I guess he thought he was the reason we were having to do it. He always went out to the barn or the back porch. It was easy to talk to Mama without Daddy around, and before I knew it, I was telling her all about Erin and her angry threat.

"I'm going to have a talk with Mrs. Sawyer Sunday after service," she said without looking up from her sewing.

I let mine fall to the floor. "No, Mama, please! Don't. You'll make Erin madder at me than she already is."

"Nonsense. I'm not trying to get her in trouble, but her mother needs to know she's behaving this way. I don't know Mrs. Sawyer very well, as they haven't been here long, but she seems a reasonable woman. I'm sure she'd rather know than not. I certainly would."

I picked up my sewing and restarted. There was no sense in trying to convince Mama otherwise.

*She made up her mind, and that was that. It was
times like those that I figured I didn't get all my
stubbornness from Daddy. Some of it came from
Mama.*

*Sunday morning came, church service went,
and there we were—Mama, Mrs. Sawyer, Erin,
and me—all standing in a small circle facing one
another. Daddy and Mr. Sawyer were walking the
Hinkles to their car.*

*"I'd like to talk to you about something, if you
don't mind, Mrs. Sawyer," Mama began.*

*My gut wrenched up into a ball. There was no
getting out of it now. Erin sneered at me. Part of
me, a little part, felt sorry for her. But the other
part of me, the bigger part, wanted to yank her
braids.*

Mrs. Sawyer nodded. "Go right ahead."

*"Well," Mama went on, "it's about Erin. She
seems to be quite unhappy about Lizzie's grades at
school, and I felt we should get things worked out."*

*Mrs. Sawyer huffed and put her arm around
Erin's shoulders. "I'm afraid the problem, my dear
Mrs. Hawkins, doesn't lie with my Erin. It lies
square on the shoulders of that prideful girl
of yours."*

*Erin smirked at me. She'd known where this
was headed before it began. She'd already painted*

me as the school prisspot to Mrs. Sawyer. My sorry feeling was shrinking by the second. I could almost feel my palms wrapped around her braids.

Mama stood there blinking. I knew Mama. She wasn't expecting this reply. She'd expected a civil apology and for Erin to get a good talking-to at home. That wasn't gonna happen.

"And furthermore," Mrs. Sawyer went on, "I would make sure I'd gotten the entire story from my own daughter before I went off and meddled with the raising of anyone else's. For example, were you aware, Mrs. Hawkins, that your daughter is the biggest show-off this side of the Mississippi? How in heaven's name do you expect Erin to not want to knock her off her pedestal?"

"I do not go around showing off," I insisted.

Mama grabbed my arm. "Lizzie, hush."

Erin began to whine. "She does so. You should see the way she acts, like she's special or something. Always laughing at everybody because they can't beat her." She lifted her glasses and wiped her eyes. Then she looked at me. One corner of her mouth was turned up a tad, just enough to let me know she was going to have her way and there was nothing I could do about it. I saw that look. I saw it and I couldn't take it. I dove at her, and the next thing I knew, my hands were squeezed around two thin brown braids. Erin screamed. The few remaining churchgoers, Pastor White included, wheeled around to see what all the commotion was about.

"Elizabeth Hawkins!" Mama jerked me back. "What on earth are you doing?"

"Well, I never!" Mrs. Sawyer grabbed Erin and pushed her behind her back like she was protecting her from the devil himself. "Mrs. Hawkins, if I were you, I'd get my daughter under control before it's too late. Such behavior should not be tolerated." She spun around and the two of them marched off to their car.

That was it. The battle between Erin and me was official. She'd dared me into it when she lied about me, right to my face. I'd full-on accepted the dare when I had nerve enough to reach out and yank her hair in the churchyard. She was determined to best me. And I was determined not to let her.

Now Erin has decided she wants to best me in another way, besides grades. She wants to steal my best friend. Well, I have something to tell Erin Sawyer, and they can print it in the paper under "School News": One day I'll have my best friend and my family back, and I'll have top grades, to boot. She can count on it.

~ *Eleven* ~

Pride Goeth Before Destruction and a Haughty Spirit Before a Fall

Asking Ben for the truth turned out to be harder than I thought. I wondered if Erin had convinced him not to be friends with me anymore. Three times I went to visit him, and his ma told me either he was gone to Mr. Reed's or he was off running errands. But he wasn't. Mrs. Butler ain't the world's best liar, and I caught Ben peeping at me through the curtains once. After that, I stopped trying. If he was determined to be friends with Erin instead of me, that was his own stupidity.

Ben or no Ben, I was happy as a pig in mud to see the last day of school roll around. Since my D two weeks earlier, I'd managed to keep my grades up pretty well. I'd made a B on a history test, but all my other grades were As. What I wanted more than anything on my last day of school was to beat Erin Sawyer for top grades.

The morning dragged by as slowly as molasses in January. Miss Jones made us dust erasers, empty and wash our inkwells, sort books, and sweep the floor. At midmorning she finally instructed, "All right, children. Please take your seats and we will announce the term's top students. Afterward, we will dismiss and head outside for Field Day. The school year will officially end at noon."

The words "Field Day" brought on hoots and hollers from the boys. The girls sat quietly, but I wasn't fooled. Some of the girls were more competitive than the boys. Girls like me. And Erin.

"Quiet down, please," Miss Jones urged. The room fell silent. "Since this is the end of the year, both second- and third-place students will receive certificates of achievement, while first place will receive this blue ribbon." Miss Jones held up the ribbon and the class answered with oohs and aahs. "All three winners will also have their names printed in the town paper's "School News" column. I would like to congratulate all of you on a job well done. Now, we'll begin with third place."

The last name in the world I wanted to hear was my own. Taking care of Mama was more important than school, but keeping my grades up was important to Daddy, and I didn't want to let him down either.

Miss Jones glanced down at the paper in her hands. I balled my fists. "Harold Watson."

I inhaled deeply, realizing I'd been holding my breath. The air rushed in and soothed me, until Erin tapped my shoulder. "You know I'm getting first place this time, Hawkins," she whispered. "You remember who got extra credit and who didn't. Guess you should've apologized to me after all."

I pretended not to hear her. I watched as Harold went to the front of the room to receive his certificate. He grinned, and Erin snickered behind me. Poor Harold. His teeth were so buck he could've eaten corn through a picket fence. He got it from his daddy. It must've been a sad thing to know that out of five kids, you were the only one to get stuck with teeth like that. Maybe his brains made up for it in some way, 'cause while the rest of the Watson kids didn't have buck teeth, they didn't have Harold's brains either. You can always get teeth fixed, but Daddy always said if you ain't got brains, you're just headed up a creek with no paddle.

Harold sat back down, and Miss Jones looked once again at her paper. "Second place goes to . . ."

This was it. If I didn't hear my name now, I'd know I'd made it to first. There was no way that one D and a B would send me all the way back to fourth place. I pictured Erin waiting just as intently as me for that first letter to come from Miss Jones's mouth. Would it be "E" or "L"? I gripped my locket, praying for the "E."

Once again, God wasn't listening.

"Lizzie Hawkins."

My heart dropped like a dead duck. I didn't want to stand up. Didn't want to go up to the front of the room and pretend to be happy about second place. But I did. Daddy had always told me to be the best in everything I did, but Mama had taught me to never be a sore loser. I stood up. I walked up to the front of the room. I smiled about second place. I did it for Mama. I did it for her, even though my insides were twisted in all the wrong ways, because I knew exactly who'd gotten first.

"Congratulations, Lizzie," Erin whispered when I sat back down. "Now, you'd best congratulate me when I'm announced. It's nice to think about all the people who'll see my name printed above yours in the paper."

I held my locket. It was cold and hard in my palm. I squeezed it tighter. *I'm sorry, Daddy. I'm sorry I let you down.*

Miss Jones's voice broke my thoughts. "And now for first place. The student with the highest grade average is . . . Erin Sawyer."

Erin let out a squeal behind me. The shrillness pierced my eardrums. I would've been disappointed to lose to anybody. But losing to Erin was devastating.

Since the beginning of 1931, all it'd done was pour rain in my life. First Ben's pa died; then I failed the spelling bee last March; then Daddy lost his job in July. If that wasn't enough, bratty old Erin had come at the start of the school year and Daddy had left before it even had the chance to end. Then a part of Mama left too. Now this. I was beginning to think the rain would never stop.

Erin took her ribbon from Miss Jones and smiled. Her teeth, unlike Harold's, were perfectly straight and white.

I guess I noticed because it was the first time I'd actually seen her smile that big. Well, if the only time she wanted to smile was when she beat me, that smile was about to disappear. We still had Field Day races to run, and before the day was through, I'd have some blue ribbons of my own.

"Let's have one last round of applause for all our hardworking students," Miss Jones said. The class erupted into rowdy claps and hollers. "And now," Miss Jones yelled above the noise, "you're dismissed to Field Day."

Kids bolted from the classroom and onto the field like ants pouring out of a stomped-on ant bed. Miss Jones and the other teachers began to organize the races. Field Day was the one day we all got to wear our regular clothes to school. Nobody, not even the most proper of teachers, expected us girls to high-jump or race in a dress.

The school competed in sections: first through third grades, fourth through sixth grades, seventh and up. The only race that required boys and girls to run separately was the 100-yard dash.

First up was the three-legged race. Ben had always been my partner before, and we'd won every year since third grade. All the other teams in our section were boy-boy or girl-girl. Even though I knew it was the combination of me and Ben together that helped us win every year—we were coordinated with each other and we both had a good sense of timing from so much fishing—I didn't want to break the tradition of my girl-boy team.

"You want to partner with me for the three-legged race?" I asked Charlie Martin. He was the tallest boy in our division, which meant he had long legs for covering a lot of ground. And he was fast. He always took the blue ribbon in the boys' 100-yard dash.

"Sure, Lizzie," he said. "Maybe then I'll have a chance to win it this year."

"Thanks, Charlie," I said. "I just can't see running it with a girl."

He laughed, and we bent down to tie the rope around our legs. "I can't see you runnin' it with a girl either."

We stood and hobbled to the line. Hobbling up to our right was Erin. She'd partnered up with Sheriff Dawson's daughter Eliza. She was two grades below us, and I figured Erin was trying to cozy up to her so it'd be easy for her to hold Sheriff Dawson over my head too, just like she did Dr. Heimler.

Erin glared at me and I glared right back. Poor Eliza Dawson didn't realize who she'd agreed to get tied up with. The grades might've gone to Erin, but the races would be mine.

"On your mark," Miss Jones called out.

Six pairs standing at the starting line wrapped their arms around each other.

"Get set."

Six pairs leaned forward, waiting for the word. . . .

"Go!"

Charlie and I took off. Our legs glided over the ground

in long, smooth strides. The pair to our left got tangled up and hit the dirt. Erin and Eliza were still to our right.

"Go faster, Charlie!" I yelled, though my legs were already struggling to keep up with his.

And faster he went. I'd never run that fast with Ben. My legs near buckled beneath me. The finish line was only another ten yards away. I had to hold on. I shifted some of my weight onto Charlie's shoulders, and for a second it felt as if he were carrying me. The finish line moved closer. The two figures to our right fell behind ever so slightly.

The finish line flashed under our feet.

We came to a stop and turned just in time to see Erin and Eliza cross the line. They'd fallen all the way back to third place.

Miss Jones clapped. "I believe that was the best race I've seen yet!"

Charlie offered his hand and I shook it. He was grinning from ear to ear. "Ben or no Ben, I'm runnin' with you again next year."

Erin stomped up to Charlie. "No wonder you won. You practically carried her across the line." She flipped her braids and walked off.

Miss Jones handed me and Charlie our blue ribbons, and we pinned them to our shirts. "You'd better hurry, Lizzie," she said. "They're lining up for the girls' hundred-yard dash. As fast as you were with one leg tied to Charlie, I'm sure you'll be even faster with both legs free."

I smiled. "Yes, ma'am. I hope so."

There were seven other girls lined up with me, including Erin.

"You won't win this one, Hawkins," she snapped. "You don't have ol' Charlie-boy to carry you down the field."

"Why don't you just worry about running the race and not your mouth?"

She hushed up and got into her running position. I did the same.

The next thing I knew, Miss Jones yelled, "Go!"

And go I did.

Right past Erin. Right past everybody.

Miss Jones had said it. I could run fast with Charlie, but I could run even faster by myself. Erin didn't stand a chance. I pictured her far behind me, the dust I was kicking up blowing right in her face. The finish line was coming up fast.

"Come on, Lizzie!" I heard Charlie call from the sideline.

The wind blew into my face, and I smiled. I was beating Erin bad. She was too far behind to catch up now. I wanted to look back just to be sure.

I don't know if Mama has any proverbs about looking behind you in the middle of a race, but it ain't really such a good idea. I never got a peek at Erin. My foot hit a hole, and without Charlie there to lean on, my legs went flying out from under me. All I got to see was the grass heading straight for my face.

I heard the pounding of Erin's feet as she ran past me. I looked up and saw her bony body crossing the finish line. I put my forehead to the ground and lay there.

"Lizzie, are you all right?" Miss Jones reached to help me up.

"Yes, ma'am. I'm fine." But I wasn't fine. My knees and palms burned like they'd been set on fire, and I'd bitten my tongue. It hurt bad, but I didn't taste blood.

"Bless your heart," she said. "You were doing just fine till you hit that hole."

I nodded, then watched Miss Jones give Erin the blue ribbon that should've been—could've been—mine. Like always when I'd done something stupid, Mama's voice echoed through my head: *A haughty spirit goeth before a fall.*

And a fall I'd had. If only I'd heard that voice a few seconds sooner.

I didn't hang around much longer after that. I left with my one battered blue ribbon—one blue ribbon that should've been two—and my second-place certificate. Erin must've seen me leaving, because I hadn't yet made it past Mr. Watson's honeysuckle-covered fence when she ran up behind me on the road. "You know, watching you bite the dust was just about the best thing I've seen since I came here. Might even top seeing Myra Robinson wet her drawers. And falling to the ground doesn't seem to be the only way you fall. You're pretty good at falling in grades too. I sure do wish Ben could've seen it."

I stopped dead in my tracks and whirled around. Her words fueled the flame of anger within me, the same flame that'd sparked the day I saw her traipsing around with Ben. Words—burning, blistering words—boiled up from that flame. But I couldn't let them escape, no matter how badly I wanted to scream at her about Ben, about Mama and Dr. Heimler, about her selfish ways. Once I did, she'd have the upper hand. She'd know she'd managed to get to me, and then her never-ending threats truly never would end. And I had Mama to think about.

I breathed in. I let myself utter two words. Two tiny words that held more weight than a million. "You win."

You know how people are always saying "like mother, like daughter" or "like father, like son"? Well, at that moment I was "like mother," because just like Mama had been shocked by Mrs. Sawyer's reply outside the church, I was shocked by Erin's now.

She reached out her hand and placed it on my shoulder. She cooed, as sweetly as if she were talking to a baby, "No, Lizzie. You're wrong. I haven't won. Not yet. I've learned a lot about you since I've been here, but the most important thing I've learned is this: you might fall, but you always find a way to get back up."

My mouth might as well have been stitched shut. I didn't know what to say to her. I thought she was apologizing. I was wrong. Dead wrong.

"It seems to me," she went on, "that if I want to keep my top spot around here, I'd do best to get rid of you once and for all. I've finally bested you, Lizzie Hawkins. I've got your best friend, I've got top grades, and I plan on keeping it that way."

For once in my life I didn't have anything to say. The flame inside me erupted into a full-blown fire, but all that smoke muddled my thinking. I just stood there. Stood there and stared.

Erin started to walk away, but she stopped short and turned back. "So have you figured out how I always know the very things you don't want me to know? Well, I'll tell you: Ben. He tells me everything. I know it all, and it's only a matter of time before the whole town does too." Then she was gone.

I stood there wondering if my best friend was purposely betraying me to my worst enemy. I didn't want to believe it. But how could I not? Ben did like rattlesnakes. And how could Erin be so sure of getting rid of me? She wasn't just sure, she was downright haughty.

Well, I knew three things for certain: First, I couldn't stand around in the middle of the road worrying about Erin; I needed to tend to Mama. Second, I had some mending to deliver to Mrs. Martin, and Erin or no Erin, delivered it was gonna be. And third, there was another part to Mama's proverb: "Pride goeth before destruction, and a haughty spirit before a fall." A haughty spirit was me. I got it. And I'd taken my fall. But if I were Erin, I'd stop being so all-fired prideful before I got flat-out destroyed.

~ *Twelve* ~

Banks Lend Umbrellas When the Sun Is Shining and Ask for Them Back When It Starts to Rain

Dr. Heimler showed up again the next day. I figured he must've designated Saturdays his "Check on Rose Hawkins Day." While I still pretended not to be home, his arrival didn't give me such a panic this time. It was earlier in the morning than last time, and I hadn't yet gone outside to work on the wash. This time I knew he hadn't seen me, 'cause I was already inside. I'd also decided ahead of time not to let Mama sit on the back porch, just in case. I'd decided right. She was sitting peacefully in her chair, and the last time I checked, a wingback chair doesn't rock. Dr. Heimler knocked a couple of times before getting in his car and driving away. Later, when I went out to sweep the front porch, a piece of paper fell from the door. It read:

Mrs. Hawkins,
I've dropped by the last two Saturdays to check on you. If you'll send Lizzie to get me at your

earliest convenience, I'll be sure to come right
away. We seem to be missing each other.

> *Sincerely,*
> *Dr. Heimler*

But Dr. Heimler wasn't the only unwanted visitor that kept stopping by. There was one even worse. The one who'd started all this mess in the first place. Since school had let out, Erin didn't seem to have anything better to do but come by and bother me. She wouldn't come up to me; she'd just stand there, hovering at the end of our drive. I looked around at all I had to do—laundry, cooking, cleaning, tending to Mama—and I thought how she needed to get her cotton-pickin' self on home and tend to her own business and stop standing around my drive trying to stick her curled-up nose into mine. She'd gotten the final word the last day of school. Guess that wasn't good enough.

Her hateful glare might've driven a lesser person inside, but not me. She could pout and stare till her eyes popped out if she wanted. I wasn't about to let her know she bothered me one little bit. I'd pull a handful of pesky weeds from the vegetable garden or sweep the front porch, and I took my sweet time doing it. This was my house, and I wasn't going inside till I was good and ready. She must've been nearly as determined as me, 'cause she'd usually stay there for the better part of half an hour before giving up and stomping off.

I'd claim small victories in waiting her out, but I couldn't escape the nagging feeling that things were about to get worse. Much worse. I tried to sweep the worries into the back corner of my brain, but they refused to disappear. Fact was fact—Erin wasn't gonna give up till she got what she wanted. And what she wanted was to get rid of me.

When Tuesday morning came, it promised a bluebird day. Since it wasn't Saturday and I planned to be home most of the day, I let Mama sit on the back porch. I helped her into her rocker, and she began her forward and back rhythm. She leaned her head back and closed her eyes. The fresh air would be good for her. She hadn't been out in days—not on the days school was still in, not on Saturday because of Dr. Heimler, and not Sunday or Monday because it'd rained. I laid her book in her lap and went to the front porch to await Erin's arrival.

It'd been four days since school ended, and Erin still hadn't tired of her harassing ways. I had. I was bound and determined that the next time she showed her scowling face at the end of my drive was gonna be her last. I was gonna jerk a knot in her tail.

I didn't get the chance, because a new unwanted visitor pulled into the drive. This one was just as bad as, if not worse than, the other two. No regular car had a star symbol on the passenger door. And no regular car had a single red light mounted on the bumper. What if he'd heard about me and Mama and was coming to take me away?

I couldn't hide. I was already out for the world to see. And I couldn't run. Running makes you look guilty, and I couldn't leave Mama here by herself. He'd find her for sure when he was looking around for me.

I decided to act as calm as possible and walk right up to his car. He might've been as big as all outdoors, but at least he wasn't mean. In fact, other than his size, I'd never really understood how he'd become sheriff. He was just a big ol' baby.

Once, I'd been walking to Hinkle's to get a few things for Mama when I passed by a group of people gathered around a truck. In the middle of the group was Sheriff Dawson, bawling his eyes out. Apparently, Mr. Watson hadn't been watching where he was going and had run right over Mrs. McClain's dog. All I know is, even Mrs. McClain wasn't crying near as bad as the sheriff.

The sheriff opened his door and stepped out. He towered above me. The top of my head barely reached his belly button. He yanked at his uniform britches, trying to get them around his potbelly. "Howdy-do, Miss Lizzie. Is your mother handy? I need to see her about some papers I've got here." He fanned the two papers in his right hand.

I didn't have a choice. I lied. To the sheriff. I wasn't sure, but I thought I could go to jail for that. "Well, sir, she had a pretty bad headache this morning, so she took some aspirin and lay down. I can take the papers to her for you."

Sheriff Dawson chewed on his bottom lip. "I appreciate

that, but this is an official paper and I need your mama to sign for it. Maybe I should just come back later."

Now, I couldn't have the sheriff coming back later. What excuse would I use then? If I said Mama still had a headache, then Dr. Heimler would be called back over. I had to get the sheriff to leave the paper now. "Oh, I'll sign for it, Sheriff," I said real quick. "I'm sure she won't mind. I'll take it straight to her. Promise." I added, so he'd think I was helping him out, "Besides, I'm sure you've got much more important things to worry about than this."

Sheriff Dawson swiped his forehead with his hand-kerchief. "Well . . ."

"You just hand it to me and you can be on your way."

He handed me the papers and a pen, but by the look on his face, I was afraid he was fixin' to snatch them right back. "You can't tell anybody but your mama I let you do this, Miss Lizzie. You tell her I didn't want to disturb her."

I slapped Mama's signature onto one paper and handed it back to the sheriff. "Yes, sir. I'll tell her."

He eased back into his car, careful of his head and belly, and said, "All righty, then. Y'all have a good one."

"Yes, sir. You too." I smiled the biggest smile I could manage and waved him off.

Once he was out of sight, I ran inside and read the official letter. Each word I read was a knife stabbing into my gut. By the time I finished reading, my stomach ached and it felt hotter than blue blazes inside the house. Sweat beaded on my forehead. I looked out the window at Mama. She was rocking back and forth, her eyes still closed. It wouldn't do any good to tell her what the letter said. It might even make her worse. I had to handle it by myself. And there'd be no time to wait around on Daddy either, whether or not he showed up on my birthday. I didn't have even that much time. I had to get started on a plan this very second.

I read over the words again:

Mr. and Mrs. Hawkins:

We are sorry to inform you that you are behind on your mortgage payments. Please bring your mortgage up to date within thirty days of delivery of this letter by remitting payment in the amount of $22.50 to Bittersweet Savings and Loan.

If you fail to make this payment within thirty days, Bittersweet Savings and Loan will pursue legal action to foreclose on the mortgage, which will result in the sale of the property.

All back payments shall be added to your current mortgage payment of $22.50, bringing your new mortgage payment to a total of $33.75 for a total of six consecutive months (or 180 days). During this probationary period, no payment to Bittersweet Savings and Loan should be missed. If a missed payment occurs, Bittersweet Savings

and Loan reserves the right to begin foreclosure
proceedings.

We are happy to help you resolve this matter.
Please contact Mr. Edward V. Cooper for personal
assistance.

> *Sincerely,*
> *Daniel B. Roberts*
> *President, Bittersweet Savings and Loan*

So that was the whole of it. I had underestimated exactly how far behind Mama and Daddy had gotten on the mortgage. Reading that letter forced me to face those horrible feelings I'd felt toward Daddy the morning he left. Feelings I didn't want to face. Sharp disappointment and deep hurt. He'd known this was gonna happen before he left. And he'd still up and gone anyway. I tried to breathe out the feelings, but they stuck inside me like glue.

Still, maybe he was coming home soon. Maybe like I hoped. On my birthday. Surely he was making all kinds of money wherever he'd gone to. I bet he knew all along just how much time he had to make that money and hightail it home. But I couldn't count on it. I'd already wasted a whole month waiting on Daddy to show, and I couldn't waste another. I was the one holding the bank notice. I was the one who had to try to fix it.

~ *Thirteen* ~

Hard Work Means Prosperity; Only a Fool Idles Away His Time

My idea of how to fix it was something that I'd once sworn up and down I'd never do. I didn't know if Daddy would approve or not, but he wasn't here. I had no choice. I was going to fight any way I could, with or without Daddy. Mama needed me to. If Daddy was gonna have something to say about it, he should've been around to say it.

I hurried out to the back porch and moved Mama back inside. She struggled against me, but I couldn't help it—I had to leave, so she had to come in. As soon as she was situated, I raced down the drive and turned toward town. Toward Hinkle's.

My knees and ankles ached from my feet pounding against the ground, but I kept going, running farther and faster than I ever had.

Mr. Hinkle looked up at the sound of the bell. "Well, hello, Miss Lizzie. What can I do for you today?"

The big butterfly in my belly came back and began

fluttering around inside me, identical to the way it had the day I got my D. The outcome hadn't been good then; maybe today wouldn't be any better. I started to turn around and leave, but the thought of Mama stopped me.

"Mr. Hinkle," I said before I could chicken out.

"Yes, ma'am?"

Every muscle in my body twitched with determination to keep the question I needed to ask inside me. But I had to be stronger than that. I took a deep breath and dug way down deep, deeper than I ever thought I could, and fought against myself. I forced my mouth open, letting the words escape. "I need a job. Any job. For any pay you can spare."

There. I'd done it. And I was still breathing. Lightning hadn't struck me dead or anything. Maybe Daddy had been wrong. Asking for help wasn't *that* bad.

Mr. Hinkle froze, his eyes blinking faster than usual. He cleared his throat. "Well now, Miss Lizzie, I'd love to have you here, but it's like this: there's a depression going on, and we haven't got much money to spare. I just don't—"

"Please think about it, Mr. Hinkle." The begging was coming easier.

Mrs. Hinkle came bustling out of the back room. Mr. Hinkle stiffened at the sight of her.

"What in heaven's name are you two prattling on about? I swear I have to do everything around here. Look at you, just standing around going on about nothing all day. Injustice. That's what it is." She grabbed a few cans and stormed off into the back again.

Lord knows, I was crazy for asking to work on the same street as her, much less in the same store.

"Does everything around here?" Mr. Hinkle mumbled to himself. He looked at me, an amused grin spreading across his face. "Tell you what, I'll consider it. But you've got to give me a day or two to think it over."

Mr. Hinkle had gone crazier than a bess-bug if he thought I was leaving his store without an answer. I'd worked up the guts to ask for help, and that was a mortal sin in Daddy's eyes. I wasn't gonna spend the next few days wondering if my guts had been wasted.

"Please, Mr. Hinkle. I can't wait that long. Why don't I look around for a few minutes while you decide?" I strolled over to the candy case.

Mrs. Hinkle came back out and took a few more cans. "Elizabeth Hawkins," she screeched, "if you don't back away from that glass, you're going to be the one cleaning it."

I eased back and glanced over at Mr. Hinkle. He was slumped over the counter, his fingers plugged in his ears. I thought I could hear him mumble something, but I wasn't sure. Mrs. Hinkle disappeared into the back room again, and Mr. Hinkle summoned me over.

"All right. I've reached a decision. I'm certain you'd be one of the finest workers I'd ever hired, truly worth every penny, but . . ."

I felt the urge to jump over the counter and wring the answer out of him. "Yes?" I whispered.

"There's one thing that bothers me about this deal."

"Yes, sir."

"You see, I'd have to take a lot of grief from Mrs. Hinkle if I hired you, and I'm not altogether certain my old heart could hold up to it. But I'm still willing to chance it if you'll accept some terms."

I nodded, maybe a little too fast.

He smiled, deepening the crinkles at the corners of his eyes. "You've got to work every afternoon from twelve till four, except on Sundays. I'll pay you ten cents an hour." He eyed me. "What's your reply?"

I tried to pretend I was thinking on the matter, but I'd never been good at disguising excitement. Working at the store would give me a regular income. "I accept."

"All right. One more thing. We still don't have a deal unless . . . You listening?"

"Yes, sir."

"Unless you take one of those blasted Goo Goo Clusters you're constantly drooling over. I'm likely to start getting questions about why the glass is always wet."

I bolted around the counter and threw my arms around him. He pushed me back, attempting to be serious. "Do we have a deal?" He put out his hand.

"Yes, sir," I said, shaking it. "We have a deal."

"Good. I'll expect to see you at twelve o'clock tomorrow, and don't be late. If there's one thing the missus and I agree on, it's that we don't tolerate tardiness."

I nodded and walked out of Hinkle's happy I'd asked for a job. I never thought getting one would make me feel so good. After all, I was leaving with a regular income and a gooey Goo Goo Cluster melting slowly away in my mouth.

I'd just finished my last bite when I saw Ben coming off Oak Street onto Main. I called out to him. He waved but didn't come over. I could see why. On a leash right beside him, behaving pretty as you please, was Ziggy, and right behind them, rounding the corner, was Mr. Reed. I looked twice to be sure I wasn't seeing things. I closed my eyes and counted out the date. May 24. The time? What time was it? Just before lunch. I opened my eyes. It wasn't the first or the fifteenth. It wasn't between one o'clock and three o'clock. Yet here was Mr. Reed. In town. I watched Ben, Ziggy, and Mr. Reed walk down the street toward Henderson's Hardware. Together. For Mr. Reed to go and break his longtime habits like that, he must've really liked Ben. A lot.

That night I spent an extra-long time with Mama, reading aloud the entire "Rhyming Proverbs" section in her book. The amount of time I'd spent with her over the past two weeks had shrunk to the size of a cotton boll, and making her sit inside every time I left made me feel extra bad.

During the nightly hundred brush strokes I gave Mama's hair, I thought about my new job. It wouldn't be enough to last us. That much I knew. But it was a step—no matter how small—toward saving the house.

I reached the hundredth stroke and kept going, waiting on one of Mama's wise sayings to pop out of her head, into the brush, up my arm, and into my brain. Then I'd know what to do. Maybe if she couldn't tell me with her mouth, she could tell me with her mind.

Two hundred strokes.

Nothing.

I put the brush on Mama's nightstand, braided her hair, and helped her into bed. Maybe she was too tired to think.

In my room, even before I put on my nightgown, I pulled my journal from the drawer.

May 24, 1932

Asking Mr. Hinkle for a job today made me think of Daddy losing his last year. It was just before the Fourth of July. No time is a good time to lose a job, I know, but the man who laid Daddy off right before a national holiday should've been horsewhipped.

Daddy came home three hours early that Friday, and when Mama asked if he was feeling sick, he just said, "It was me today."

Mama gasped and covered her mouth. Even I had understood what Daddy meant. For months, the steel mill where he worked had been cutting back on wages and workers. Daddy said all the men working there had gotten real quiet at their work since the depression came on. Daddy said each day all the men just crossed their fingers and prayed that it wouldn't be them next. They figured if they stayed quiet enough, the bosses wouldn't remember they were there. And they couldn't get rid of somebody they didn't remember. Well, either Daddy got too loud or somebody remembered him.

During supper that night, my stomach was balled up in a knot and it wouldn't let my food go down. Mama kept saying things like "We'll make it work" and "We'll get by." Daddy didn't say anything. He went to bed early.

The next night, I begged and begged for Mama and Daddy to come and watch the fireworks with me. Neither of them did.

I met Ben at our usual place, right in front of Powell's. His ma wasn't there either.

Bittersweet looked beautiful with all the storefronts dressed in ribbons of red, white, and blue for the occasion. A huge banner stretched out over Main Street. It read, same as every other year: Welcome to Bittersweet's Annual Fourth of July Celebration—The Sweetest Celebration Around. *But Ben and I both knew that this particular party was more bitter than sweet.*

Before long, the eight members of the high school band were tuning up their instruments in preparation for "The Star Spangled Banner," to be played during the short fireworks show. At the mayor's signal, the first firework burst into the air. The band blasted forth their tune. And, for the first time in our lives, Ben and I sat watching the fireworks explode into the night sky without our parents beside us.

All the locals had gathered for the event and were lining Main Street up one side and down the other, packed together like sardines. With each explosion, the crowd clapped and cheered. But not Ben and me. When somebody you love is sad, that sadness rubs off on you somehow. It made all the celebrating seem cruel. Without Mama and Daddy, loneliness filled me, even with all those people around. Even with Ben right there beside me.

Over the next few weeks, nearly every time I saw Daddy he had a newspaper in his hands, searching for a job. There were none. Daddy changed. Some of the fight went out of him. Mama changed too. It was the first time I could remember that she didn't have a proverb ready and waiting to make sense of everything. Maybe the problems were too big for words.

Maybe they still are.

I thought about Ben asking for a job at Mr. Reed's and me asking for a job at Hinkle's. I thought about Mama and me going around collecting sewing and laundry from anybody who would give it after Daddy lost his job. I didn't understand. If me and Ben and Mama could find a job here, no matter how small, why couldn't Daddy? Why couldn't he have stayed?

~ *Fourteen* ~

The Sting of a Reproach Is the Truth of It

After work on Saturday, I got my very first pay from Mr. Hinkle. One dollar and sixty cents. It wasn't gonna pay the mortgage overnight, but I was happier than a lark to be earning something. Sewing, fishing, and vegetables were all well and good, but one thing was for certain— they didn't add up to enough to pay the mortgage.

When I got home, I took a canning jar from the pantry and started a savings jar all my own. The sound of the change clinking against the glass was better than music. I put the jar under my bed and went out to ask Mama what she wanted for supper.

I asked her every day, thinking she'd answer me at least once. She hadn't yet, and as I stood there watching her staring and rocking, rocking and staring, I stopped myself. She hadn't said a word in weeks, and I couldn't bear to ask another question only to hear silence in reply.

I let Mama be and went to rummage through the kitchen. I had two choices: dumplings or pancakes. I was near dumplinged out, so I decided on pancakes. Strange, yes, but easy.

I'd just cracked the eggs when there was a *tap-tap-tap* on the front door. My heart near jumped right out of my throat. I'd have known that knock anywhere. The sound of it widened the crack of hope in my mountain of hurt.

"Come in!" I called. "I'm in the kitchen."

Ben tromped in, raking his fingers through his hair. It had lightened considerably from working outdoors over the past month, going from straw to cotton. His eyebrows had all but disappeared. He was also filthy. Any of Mr. Reed's dirt that hadn't set up house on Ben's overalls was either smudged across his face or packed beneath his nails.

As dirty as he was, I wanted to fling my arms around him and tell him how much I'd missed him. But I couldn't. The memory of him coming out of Hinkle's that day with *her* was burned into my mind. And why was he finally showing up now, after he'd been avoiding me like the plague for the past two weeks? I wanted the truth, once and for all.

Ben spoke before I had the chance to demand it. "What'cha doin'?" he asked. He peered over at the pancake batter.

"Making supper for Mama."

"How is she?" He shuffled over to the window and looked out. "Dr. Heimler ever come check on her?"

"He did, several times, but I pretended I wasn't home. He hasn't been by this week. Maybe he forgot about us."

Ben shook his head. "Man alive, you're stubborn. You should've let him look at her."

"*I'm* stubborn! What about you? You're the one who refuses to believe Erin Sawyer is bad news. I saw you with her, Ben, so don't go trying to get around it. Have you been talking to her?"

"Well, so what if I have? I didn't think you'd take the time to notice." The corner of his mouth retreated inside his cheek. He heaved a breath. "I've been talkin' to Erin for a while, even before your daddy left."

"What are you saying, Ben? That you're picking her over me?" I poured a small pancake into the skillet. It sat there like a blob. Skillet needed to be hotter.

"I ain't pickin' anybody over anybody, but who else does she have to talk to? Who else do I have? The way you act sometimes makes it hard not to think about pickin' her. I think I've just about reached Wits' End Corner with *you*, Lizzie."

"With me? Listen, Ben, if Erin Sawyer doesn't have any friends, it's her own fault, and you know it. She came here mean as a rattlesnake and she just got meaner. You don't believe she's really your friend, do you? 'Cause she's only talking to you to get at me. You trying to get at me too?"

"I ain't never lied to you, Lizzie, not once. And I'm gonna tell you the truth now. I talk to Erin because she listens to me. After Daddy died, you got to where all you cared about was me being here for you. That don't seem fair."

I couldn't believe what I was hearing. My cheeks started to burn. "Sometimes I think you've got feathers for brains. Believe what you want, but the only reason she's listening to you is to find out things she's got no business knowing. How could you tell her about me and Mama, Ben?" Once I'd admitted out loud that Ben was the reason Erin knew all that she did, it pushed up the hurt inside me. It flooded through me fast and hard, drowning out all my anger. Nobody would think it, but hurt is stronger than anger.

"I didn't set out to tell her. It just happened. She'd talk, and I'd talk. Mostly about me. But then about you. But I didn't tell her nothin' else about you after she got so mad about the essay contest. I told her she was taking things too far, and she told me she was gonna drop it. She knew I was worried about you, but she said you didn't seem none too worried about me. And you didn't. I knew you saw me with her that day. She saw you staring at us from behind that car."

The pancake began to sizzle in the skillet. I flipped it and poured in another. I thought back to that day and Erin glancing over in my direction. So she *had* seen. "Well, she didn't drop it, Ben. She got worse."

Ben cleared his throat. "I tried to tell you all this that day we saw Dr. Heimler, but you were too busy rambling on about the Hinkles. And after we saw the doctor, you were worried about your mama. But it don't matter. We won't be fussin' about Erin anymore after today anyway."

"So, you finally decided to see the light and stop being friends with her?"

"No. Me and Ma's leaving."

"Well, where are you going? You still gonna ignore me when you get back?"

"We ain't comin' back. Bank's takin' the house. Got to be out in three days. We're headin' down to Montgomery to stay with my aunt."

Ben inched closer. The same blunt, breathless pain I'd felt when Daddy left gripped my insides. Ben was leaving. He was leaving me. I couldn't let him. I needed him. I always had.

"You can't move away!" I shouted. My voice erupted louder than I'd intended.

"Can't help it." Ben looked me dead in the face. "We'll have no place to live. You want us livin' like hobos?"

"No, but there has to be another way. Can't your ma talk to the banker? I mean, you just need more time, right?"

"Done tried that. Mr. Cooper's given us more time already. Time's up. We can't afford the house no more, and we all know it. I especially hate it for Mr. Reed. He's got to where he's talkin' to me pretty good now. When I leave, he'll be right back to his old ways."

The pancakes sizzled furiously. "Mr. Reed? What about me? You can't leave me. You started all this mess with

Erin, and you got to help me end it. And the bank's after our house too. Got a letter from the sheriff just this week. Suppose I can't get the money in time. You know what'll happen quick as a flash—Erin keeps at her plan, the bank takes the house, the doctor takes Mama, and the orphanage takes me. Please, Ben, don't leave me alone. Fight. For my sake." I was desperate, grasping for words that might make him try.

He threw up his hands. "Dang it, Lizzie! This ain't all about you. It's always about warring and winning to you. When are you gonna see that life ain't one big war to win? Bad things happen, good things happen. Ain't nothin' you can do to stop it any more than I could stop what happened to Pa."

"Fine. Get mad. Give up. Go have a nice life with your aunt!"

Ben grabbed my arms, his eyes blazing. "Lizzie, I don't want to hurt your feelings, but you're the most selfish person I know. You didn't hear a word I just said. You wouldn't care about my leavin' a lick if your daddy was still here, 'cause then you wouldn't need me. If you'd listened to me sooner and opened your eyes, you could've seen this comin'. But like Erin said, you're always too concerned with yourself to care about anybody else. And what's worse than being selfish is you're scared."

I jerked away from his grip, away from that word. I knew I was afraid, but I hated hearing it out loud. "Scared? Of what?"

"I reckon that's for you to figure out."

Unwanted tears stung my eyes. I struggled to hold them back. "Just go, Ben, if that's what you want to do. I'm tired of your badgering. Just leave me alone."

"Fine. Alone is what you're about to be."

Ben stormed out of the kitchen to the front door. "Oh, yeah," he called. "I almost forgot." He stomped back into the kitchen, the window rattling with each step. "Happy birthday. Didn't know when else I might see you."

He reached into his back pocket and slammed a home-made slingshot onto the table. Then he was gone. Part of me wanted to run after him and tell him I was sorry, that he was right. But a bigger part of me, the stubborn part, wouldn't let me. And so I stood there, alone, in piercing silence.

I picked up the slingshot and turned it over in my hands, running my fingers across the rough wood and smooth rubber. It looked just like Ben's, maybe better. I loved it. And hated it. It was a painful reminder that I'd forgotten Ben's birthday just two days earlier. I'd never forgotten Ben's birthday before. Had he told Erin about his birthday? Had she remembered?

A sharp smell filled the kitchen. I rushed over to the stove and flipped the pancakes. Burned. I took them out to Mama anyhow. It wouldn't matter.

"Here you go," I said as I put the plate on the table beside her. "At least they'll fill you up."

She sat stone still, not even blinking.

"Mama?"

Nothing. Not a breath. Silence. That silence frightened me more than Erin and Ben and being poor combined. It meant I was alone. Truly alone. I gripped my locket, wishing, praying, begging for Daddy to come home and make things right.

Come on, Lizzie. Don't give up. Were those my words or Daddy's? I wasn't sure.

I knelt on the dusty boards beside Mama's rocker and rested my head in her lap, just as I had many times before when I was sick or upset. I sat there thinking of Ben and everything he'd said. Thinking of how he'd told me I'd be alone. And now I was, even with Mama beside me. I sat like that till the sun sank behind the trees, waiting for her to stroke my hair and tell me everything would be all right.

~ *Fifteen* ~

The Days Are Prolonged and Every Vision Faileth

May 30. My birthday. My twelfth birthday. I tried forcing myself into feeling as sunny on the inside as the day was outside. I never would've imagined I'd be spending it without Daddy. My sixtieth maybe, but not my twelfth.

Still, it's an unwritten rule that birthdays are special days when nothing goes wrong or brings you down. It's the one day of the year when God grants you a wish. And today He was gonna grant one of mine. I felt it in my bones. And if God didn't, surely Daddy wouldn't let me down.

I spent the better part of the morning with Mama. About every two minutes I'd pray, "Please, God, please. Make her well. It *is* my birthday, you know."

I read two sections of her book aloud, sitting cross-legged next to her rocker on the back porch. The breeze lapped at the pages of Mama's book as if it were too impatient to wait on me to turn the page. About halfway through my reading, Mama stopped staring, leaned her head back against the rocker, and closed her eyes. She was listening to me. I could tell.

When I finished, I figured I'd carry on with the tradition of fishing on my birthday. Though Daddy wasn't with me, the weather was perfect, and I couldn't help but think about the possibility of landing One-Eye again. I told Mama to watch me from the porch and I'd be sure to land her a big one. She didn't open her eyes.

A warm breeze drifted through the field, sending the grass into gentle swirls and waves. Ripples danced across the water, creating millions of shimmers on its surface. I'd never been one for fairy tales, but that was how I thought it should look in a fairyland. And if there was ever a time for impossible things to happen, it was in a fairyland on your birthday.

I found the fattest cricket I could, clutched my locket, then cast out my line. I stood in silence for a while. It was quieter than I was used to. Too quiet. Most times before, either Daddy or Ben had fished with me. Silence was possible with Daddy, depending on his mood, but Ben didn't understand the meaning of the word. If he wasn't talking, he was destroying the peace by popping his slingshot.

The sick feeling I had when I thought about Daddy worsened when I thought about Ben. I didn't want our friendship to end the way Mama's and Mrs. Butler's had, but I didn't know how to stop it.

It's funny how something that usually gets on your

nerves is the very thing you miss if you can't have it, and right then I wished more than anything I could hear Ben snapping that slingshot. But I couldn't. I started to head back to the house for mine so I could pop its band, but the fishing line twitched and I stopped. Something was testing the bait.

I eased up to the edge of the water. The sky's reflection hid the fish from view.

The line twitched again, harder than before. This was it. Every cell in my body screamed that I was about to land One-Eye again. I glanced back at the porch. It made me happy to know Mama was there.

My line jerked, and the pole dug into my hands. I jerked back to set the hook. Gooseflesh covered my body as One-Eye began the battle of tug-of-war. He'd tug, but I tugged harder. I pictured him beneath the water, trying his hardest to swim to the pond's mucky bottom. I stepped back as I reeled, shortening the amount of line he had. His splashes sent water flying into the field.

One-Eye, One-Eye, One-Eye, my heart pounded in rhythmic beats. I gave a final heave and the catfish's heavy body slid out of the water. The sun glinted off his smooth, wet skin, and I raced up to inspect him.

His eyes. I had to see his eyes. I looked.

Two. Two eyes.

It was just a regular catfish, a fish anyone would've been proud to land, and it'd make a tasty dinner, but it wasn't One-Eye.

I turned to Mama, halfway expecting to see a disappointed expression plastered across her face, but she wasn't even looking in my direction. For the first time since Daddy left, I had the overwhelming feeling that maybe Mama didn't *want* to look at me. That somehow, even in her other world, she knew I'd fail to save us, just as I'd failed to catch One-Eye for the second time.

Panic rushed over me like a wave. I dropped to my knees, right there in the middle of the field. "Please, God. I can't do this alone anymore. I can't. I need a sign. Something to prove Daddy's coming home."

Like Ben had done the first day he'd plowed without his pa, I ran inside and grabbed my slingshot, along with the bottomless tin can I used as a biscuit cutter. I sat that can up on an old stump out in the field, and just like Ben had, I told myself if I shot it off ten times, Daddy was on his way home. I searched around for twelve rocks, allowing two extra since I'd never shot a slingshot before. I put the rock in the sling the way I'd watched Ben do hundreds of times; then I pulled it back and let it go. It dropped to the ground only a few feet in front of me. Eleven more times, the same thing happened. I wasn't getting my sign. Only thing left to do was pray. Pray hard.

But though I could pray till the sun went down, facts were facts. The feeling my wish was gonna come true had vanished the second I spotted that two-eyed catfish. And there was no tricking it back, either.

I spent the better part of half an hour sprawled out in

the field, trying to invent some way of making my life, our life, better. Fast. But there was no way. I was happy to have my job at Hinkle's, and my odd mending jobs, but they weren't enough to rescue us completely. I'd wasted too much time waiting around on Daddy to come back.

I opened my locket to examine the faces inside but quickly snapped it shut. I couldn't face the deep disappointment that gripped me when I looked into Daddy's dark eyes.

I pushed the feeling aside, grasping at the last pinprick of hope. I picked up the stringer that held my two-eyed catfish and trudged to the end of our drive, the sun beating down on the dusty road. Over and over in my head I repeated: *Please let there be. Please let there be. Please let there be.*

The mailbox's handle felt cold and hard inside my grasp. The box screeched as I opened it. Slowly, I reached inside and shuffled through the little mail we'd gotten, searching for Daddy's perfect penmanship.

Nothing.

I shoved the mail back into the box and slammed the door. "What are you doing?" I screamed at my locket as though Daddy could hear. I couldn't understand. He'd always been there. Why wasn't he now, when we needed him most?

Time ticked past. Each second moved the bank deadline closer and closer. First things first. It was edging on close to noon, and I needed to get to Hinkle's. Even the smallest earnings counted for something. Seconds spent working were seconds spent well.

Still, I'd need more money than that. And money wasn't easy to come by. The only money I knew of was in Mama and Daddy's emergency savings jar. Well, if Daddy failed to show, this would count as an emergency, wouldn't it?

I ran back to the house, straight into the kitchen, dropped my fish into the sink, and retrieved the money jar from the cabinet. It felt heavy in my hands. Maybe there was more in it than I'd thought. Maybe it was just the weight of the Mason jar. I turned it bottom up, spilling its contents onto the counter. Loose change rolled off and clanged on the floor. I shook the jar again. A small wad of bills dropped out. I smoothed them, picked up the change, and counted. Eleven dollars and fifty-eight cents. Plus the dollar sixty from Mr. Hinkle, and zero dollars zero cents left from my mending work. That money had gone straight to the electric bill. That left me with a grand total of $13.18. A little less than ten dollars more would pay the mortgage for now. Maybe I could work some extra hours at Hinkle's or . . .

Or what? I wasn't sure, but I knew I needed to get on with figuring it out. I stuffed the money back into the jar and put it back in its secret spot behind the plates.

My mind whirled with ideas as I cleaned my fish and put the wrapped pieces into the icebox. With noon fast approaching, I hurried onto the back porch to get Mama.

She pulled against me when I tried to move her inside. She'd resisted me a little on days past, but this was different. She wanted to stay outside, and that was the way it was going to be whether I liked it or not. Since it was a Monday, I let her have her way. Dr. Heimler had yet to show on a Monday. Besides, it would only be for a few hours, and then I'd be home. I kissed Mama's cheek and took off.

If the sunny weather was attempting to predict a good day, it was flat-out wrong. I hadn't been at work for more than two hours when Erin flounced in. I was standing at the back dusting off shelves of jams and jellies when I heard her high-pitched voice echo through the store.

"Hello, Mr. Hinkle. How are you today?"

"Why, Erin, I'm fine as frog hair. You?"

"I'm fine. I just came in to get a few things for Mother."

"All righty. You just hand me the list and I'll let you know when I've finished."

Mr. Hinkle might've been fine as frog hair when Erin came in, but he probably wouldn't be so lucky by the time she went out. And if he was, I figured I wouldn't be. Unless I hid. If Erin couldn't see me, she couldn't bother me. I ducked into the back room with Mrs. Hinkle.

"What are you doing back here?" Mrs. Hinkle shrieked. "I gave you a dust rag not ten minutes ago, and you're supposed to be using it." She pointed her fat finger toward the storefront.

Erin was waiting for me when I came back out.

"What'cha hiding from, Lizzie?" Erin whispered. "Wouldn't be me, would it?"

"Go away, Erin," I said. "I'm busy."

Erin's eyes widened at the realization that I was an employee, not a customer. "You mean you're working here? Things must be pretty bad for that to happen."

"Everything's fine. Now, will you get your mother's things and go?" I turned around and began to dust, carefully picking up one jelly jar at a time, wiping the wood beneath it, and putting it back.

"All finished, Erin," Mr. Hinkle called from the front counter.

Erin didn't budge. She watched me work for a few seconds before she said in a hushed voice, "I'm going. You just be careful not to drop anything."

I ignored her and picked up another jar. The next thing I knew, Erin's shoulder rammed straight into the middle of my back. The force shoved me into the shelf, and I grabbed hold of it, trying to steady myself. It jerked and jiggled against my weight. Two jars teetered and crashed to the floor. Shattered glass and blueberry jam burst across the wood floor like a giant, sparkling ink blot.

I turned to give Erin a piece of my mind, but she was already taking her bag from Mr. Hinkle.

Mrs. Hinkle came flying out of the back room. "Land sakes, you careless girl! You'd best get to cleaning that up this instant! And don't you think for one minute that I won't take the cost of that jam out of your pay." She mumbled something else I couldn't make out, and then hurried away.

Erin smirked at me as she went out the door. Mr. Hinkle brought over a mop and patted my shoulder. "Accidents happen," he said. "I've knocked over more than my fair share of jars in my time." He glanced up to make sure Mrs. Hinkle was in the back again. "I always got in trouble too."

I wanted to tell Mr. Hinkle that this wasn't an accident. That Erin had caused me to do it. But it was useless. In front of all the adults in town, she was as sweet as pie. It was people her own age who got to see her as sour as unripe persimmons.

The rest of the afternoon dragged by at a snail's pace. I tried to stay extra quiet and extra careful. Mrs. Hinkle was already madder than a wet hen, and I didn't want to make it worse.

When it was finally time for me to escape Mrs. Hinkle's watchful eyes, I was sorry to see another pair of eyes watching for me. Once again, Erin was standing just outside the door.

"Well, if it isn't Little Orphan Annie."

"What do you want now?" I asked as I moved around her. "You should have to pay for those jars of jam."

"You should learn to be more careful. Besides, you don't need to worry about paying for those jars. You won't be around long enough to even see your next payday."

I faced her. My throat tightened. "Lucky for me, I'll be seeing lots of paydays, because I'm not going anywhere."

She laughed. "Sure you are. Don't you want to know where?"

I pushed past her. "Go home, Erin. You're wasting my time."

She grabbed my shirt and yanked me back. "You're a flat-out liar, and you know it!"

"I'm sick of this, Erin. You can't hurt me, so quit acting like you can. If you could, you'd have done it before now. So go home." I started walking as calmly as I could, but inside my chest my heart was flipping and flopping around like a fish out of water. Something was different. Erin had gotten her proof. I knew it.

"Don't walk away from me," she called. "I had to stay with Mother after church yesterday. She's helping to get a charity drive together for the town needy. Mr. Cooper from the bank was there, and he nominated three families he hadn't received mortgage payments from in a couple months. Yours was one of them. Said he'd just sent a letter out to your mama last week."

That loudmouthed banker. Didn't he know it wasn't professional to go around announcing his customers' business to the entire church congregation? I wasn't God or anything, but I didn't think he'd exactly go to heaven for that.

"And that's not all," Erin continued. "He said if any of you missed another payment he'd have to take your houses away, same as he had to do to Ben." Erin's voice softened when she said the part about Ben—softened enough to make me believe that somewhere in that hard shell of a girl was a person with *some* feelings.

I didn't ponder it for long. Rage rushed through me. How could Mr. Cooper do that when he sat in church every Sunday singing hymns and saying his prayers? Taking people's houses away definitely was not a Christian thing to do.

"And you're happy we might lose our house?" I snapped.

"I am when it concerns you getting what you deserve. Before we came here I was dumb enough to believe any lie that sounded half true." Her jaw tightened. "I was too weak to stand up for myself. I vowed I'd never be that way again. And I meant it. I'm gonna be something someday. I'm gonna be better than all of them. Better than you. Everybody who ever lied to me or pushed me around will be sorry."

Erin's face displayed a stubborn determination I hadn't witnessed on anyone except Daddy. For once the expression didn't inspire me, it frightened me.

"You're a spoiled, selfish brat, Erin Sawyer. Now leave me alone before I make you wish you hadn't been born."

"Oh, no, I'm not done yet. Since I knew you were working, I went by your house to check on your mama. She didn't answer the door, but I'm sure you know where I found her. On the back porch. I went up to talk to her. . . ." Erin leaned in close to me, pretending she didn't want anyone else to hear. "But I don't have to tell you the rest, because we both know you're smart enough to figure it out on your own."

Thoughts and emotions pulsed through me. They crashed into each other, forming new feelings I'd never known—panic, terror, and a dark fear that my life was about to change forever. How could I have been so stupid, letting Mama stay outside? She didn't know what was good for me anymore. How could she possibly know what was good for herself? I was being punished—punished for my stupidity.

Erin grinned. "Don't look so worried. I know from Ben that it's your birthday, and I'll be over this afternoon with your present, a gift straight from the church charity drive. I hope your mother feels up to visitors."

She pranced off down the street. *Let her prance the whole way home,* I thought. *She doesn't know who she's messing with.*

I had no doubt she would be back, but the question was, who would be with her? Her snoopy mother, snitchin' Mr. Cooper, Sheriff Dawson? Maybe all of them. And they'd all be alert, ogling Mama's condition, looking for any reason I'd be better off at Brightside Orphanage.

Erin had gotten her proof, and now I needed mine. Proof that I could take care of me and Mama. Erin Sawyer had gone flat-out nuts if she thought for one second that I was gonna let her convince people I was better off at some orphanage, bright side or not.

~ *Sixteen* ~

By Land or Water, the Wind Is Ever in My Face

I stood in the doorway watching Mama. As far as anyone in town was concerned, the thing that made Mama crazy was that she never went to church anymore. Forget that she never went *anywhere* anymore. Same thing happened to Mrs. Butler. She stopped going to church, and suddenly she was insane. Of course, no one ever said that to her face, but I overheard many a whisper in the church pews on Sunday mornings after Mr. Butler died.

I once asked Mrs. Butler why she didn't go anymore. "I don't see much point in praising God for taking away my family's only chance at survival," she'd said.

When I'd told Mama what she said, Mama's eyes had gotten real big. "I don't want you listening to that kind of talk. You understand me? Louise isn't in her right mind just now."

I told Mama I understood, but I didn't think there was anything crazy about what Mrs. Butler had said. She was hurt, that was all.

Mama went over to have a "talk" with Mrs. Butler the very next day. Ben heard it all from his room—Mama telling Mrs. Butler she ought not say such things; Mrs. Butler saying that Mama didn't know what it felt like to lose her husband. Mrs. Butler refused to take back what she'd said, and Mama refused to accept that. When Mama came home, I could tell she'd been crying. She wouldn't talk about it, and she and Mrs. Butler stopped being close after that. It's strange how so-called Christian folk, like Mama, end up deserting the ones who need them most. But I reckon a lot of folks are funny like that. They get so worried about being right, they end up doing wrong.

Ben told me he'd once caught his ma crying in her room. She'd tried to hide it, but when Ben asked her what was wrong she'd said she was alone and no one in the world cared. I pictured all the people in church on Sundays, whispering about Mama now instead of Mrs. Butler. I watched Mama, and I wondered if she and Mrs. Butler could be friends again, even though Mama had been so unkind.

I walked over to the rocker and squatted down. "Mama?" I whispered. I gently touched her arm. My skin appeared darker against her paleness.

The breeze had blown long strands of hair into her face. I tucked them behind her ear. "Mama?" I said, louder this time.

The *rumm-rumm, rumm-rumm* of the rocker against the wood continued. My throat burned as I fought back the pool of tears that jumbled and blurred Mama. *Look at her, Daddy! Look what you've done! Why did you leave? You could've stayed. You should've.* All the thoughts I'd struggled to fight back every day after Daddy left came flooding out. Pain throbbed from my clenched fists, my knuckles white and ridged beneath my skin. I wiped the stream of tears from my cheeks.

"Don't worry, Mama," I whispered. "Everything'll be all right."

I hurried inside to straighten the house. Everything had to be perfect. People who claim something is wrong will look for any reason, no matter how small, to say they're right. That was exactly what I expected from my visitors.

I didn't have long to ready things. A knock at the door signaled that my time was up.

"Who is it?" I called, dreading the reply.

"Church charity. May we come in?" The voice was sickeningly sweet, dripping with honeyed venom. Mrs. Sawyer.

"Just a second." I took a deep breath that did little to calm my nerves, then opened the door. "Please, come in."

I welcomed the visitors one by one: Mrs. Sawyer, Erin, and finally Mr. Cooper. I tried to do it just as Mama had done many times before. She called it "receiving guests."

Three pairs of eyes began darting around in all directions, sizing up their surroundings. These weren't guests; they were a bunch of meddling ninnies.

"Please, have a seat," I instructed, motioning toward the parlor.

"Thank you," said Mrs. Sawyer. She perched her round body on the edge of Mama's wingback chair, steadying herself in the find-out-what-I-can-and-get-out position. "We felt," she went on, "we should check on you, Elizabeth. Mr. Cooper said you all had been having a hard time since your daddy disappeared. Any word from him?"

One thing was clear. She wasn't wasting any time with getting into her prying questions. Erin smirked at me from her mother's side, and Mr. Cooper nodded as though I should be grateful for his interference.

"No, ma'am," I said. "Not yet."

"Not yet! Young lady, it's been two months!"

Mr. Cooper leaned closer to me. "Don't worry. We're here to help."

Mrs. Sawyer shifted. "Yes, well, the type of help you need hasn't quite been decided, but we brought you some canned items from the church food drive to hold you over: Mrs. Martin's prizewinning pear preserves, some sugar courtesy of Hinkle's General Store, and two quarts of my special bread-and-butter pickles." She patted her pickles, then passed me the basket.

"Thank you." I stood, hoping they'd take a hint and get the heck out. But Erin wasn't gonna let me off that easy.

"Don't you think we ought to speak to Mrs. Hawkins before we go?" Erin asked. She nudged her mother, and I knew that Mrs. Sawyer had already gotten an earful from Erin about her visit with Mama earlier.

"She's fine," I said quickly. "She's on the porch resting. She isn't feeling well and doesn't like visitors seeing her looking so poorly. You understand."

"It's no wonder she isn't feeling well," said Mrs. Sawyer. "I can't imagine how I'd feel if my husband had left me. We might do her some good. Visits can help cure what ails you like nothing else. Besides, it'd be rude of us not to see her."

Mr. Cooper couldn't resist throwing his unwanted opinion into the discussion. "Absolutely."

"No, I really think it'd be best if—"

"Nonsense, Elizabeth," said Mrs. Sawyer, bumping me out of her way. "Now behave yourself. This is no way to treat charitable neighbors who come to call."

Mrs. Sawyer reached for the doorknob and turned it. Hurried prayers for Mama to be miraculously healed, for Mrs. Sawyer to pass out cold, for the world to end raced through my mind. The room started to spin around me, paralyzing me where I stood. I watched as three vultures made their way out to prey on Mama.

"Hello, Rose. How are you today?" Mrs. Sawyer's shrill voice shattered the heavy air.

I rushed out to stand beside Mama. Mr. Cooper bent over into her line of sight.

"We hope we're not intruding," he said, "but it is so good to see you."

Mama stared through Mr. Cooper, her eyes fixed on the invisible scene at the pond. Mrs. Sawyer glanced out at the pond, then back at Mama.

God, she's all I have left. Don't take her away from me.

"Are you all right, Mrs. Hawkins?" Mr. Cooper asked. He gently tapped Mama's hand, trying to make eye contact. "Can you hear us?"

Mama didn't acknowledge Mr. Cooper's question or his touch. Her rocking persisted in the silence. *Rumm-rumm, rumm-rumm, rumm-rumm.* Mrs. Sawyer was, as usual, the first to open her mouth.

"Elizabeth Hawkins! Your mother needs a doctor."

Mr. Cooper wasn't gonna miss his second opportunity to put in his opinion. "I agree entirely."

Erin stood beside her mother, scrutinizing my every move. She knew I was panicking, and after she watched me suffer through the next few minutes of discussion concerning Mama's condition, she decided to up the stakes.

"Poor, poor, Lizzie," she said, running to my side and wrapping her arms around me. "How can you stand to live here with your father gone and your mother ill like this? How do you make it all on your own?"

Mr. Cooper and her mother were now staring at me— Mr. Cooper with pity and concern, Mrs. Sawyer with sharp disapproval. Erin had successfully planted a seed of doubt in their minds, a doubt that I had any business living in my own home under such circumstances.

Quivers rattled my stomach. I fought to keep them

from erupting through my voice. "Mama doesn't have a condition. She misses Daddy. I told you she didn't feel like visitors."

Mr. Cooper put his hand on my shoulder. "People do miss loved ones when they leave, but sometimes it consumes them to the point they no longer function. That seems to be the case with your mother."

"Yes," said Mrs. Sawyer, "and when that happens, it's best to seek medical assistance. Your mother looks perfectly well on the outside, but she's not well at all on the inside."

"I know!" said Erin. "Why don't we bring Dr. Heimler over to examine Mrs. Hawkins?"

"No one can afford extra doctor bills right now," I argued. I glared at Mr. Cooper. "I'm sure you know bills are already hard enough to pay without them."

Erin smiled and placed an insincere hand on my shoulder. I wanted to slap it right back off. "That's true," Erin said. "I can't see how you pay any bills without your mama or daddy working, but money won't be a problem because Dr. Heimler will examine your mother for free. Haven't you seen the sign posted on his front door?"

I shook my head, praying it was a trick and there wasn't any sign on Dr. Heimler's door. I didn't know if there truly was, since I avoided Dr. Heimler's house like it would disease me.

"Yes," said Mrs. Sawyer. "It reads: *Offering Reduced Charges or Free Services to Those with a Need. Inquire*

Within. I've already spoken to him once about your mother. Has he never come to see about her?"

I decided it was best to ignore the part about her calling Dr. Heimler on Mama. "Please," I said. "I don't think she needs him."

"Look at your mama! We simply won't take no for an answer."

Erin looked at me, her eyes dark and cold. "You're not afraid of what the doctor might say, are you, Lizzie? I mean, it's only the worst crazies that get sent off, and even if that happens, you'll get to go live somewhere else for a while. It'll take a lot of worries off you."

I grabbed the front of Erin's dress and yanked her close. "Listen here, you pigheaded brat, my mama's not crazy. And I'm not going anywhere. Just you try and make me!"

"Elizabeth Hawkins! Take your hands off my daughter this instant." Mrs. Sawyer glared at me with a look that could've melted ice. "Hasn't your mother taught you any manners? We come here offering help and this is the thanks we get. I'm going for the doctor *and* the sheriff immediately. I can only imagine what living in this situation must be doing to a girl your age. Your mother isn't so high and mighty now, is she?"

"You don't know anything about Mama!" I shouted. "I'm not in a situation, and I never asked for your help. I don't need it, and neither does Mama. Now get out!"

"You'd best ready yourself," Mrs. Sawyer said, pointing her finger in my face, "because your life is about to change whether you want it to or not. Mr. Cooper, you stay here with them. We'll be back shortly."

Erin shoved past me. She didn't say anything. She didn't have to. The meaning in her push was apparent—salt in the open wound she'd inflicted upon me.

Mr. Cooper moved aside to let the "ladies" pass. I couldn't read his face. He walked over to me and patted my head like I was a two-year-old. "I'm sorry, Lizzie," he whispered, "but something must be done. For both your sakes."

~ Seventeen ~

He Who Makes a Mouse of Himself
Will Be Eaten by the Cats

It was over. A sick, uncontrollable feeling of absolute failure swept over me. Dr. Heimler, the sheriff, Brightside
Orphanage, all of it careening closer with each passing
second.

I closed my eyes, imagining my arms wrapped around
Daddy. Comfort didn't come. It'd been too long since I'd
seen his face, heard his voice. He wasn't there, and there
was no use trying to pretend he was.

But even in defeat, my stubborn nature refused to die.
I knew I had to keep fighting, and keep fighting I would.
For Mama.

Mr. Cooper cleared his throat and attempted to make
small talk with Mama by asking her about the book she
was holding. He didn't succeed. I almost felt sorry for
him. He nervously tapped his right foot and fiddled with
his collar. I'd gotten used to Mama's silence. But I could
see that it made Mr. Cooper uneasy.

I tried to be brave. I mustered up all the gumption I could, trusting myself to think of something to get us out of this mess. I spoke steadily. "I'm about to fix some supper. Care for anything?"

I feared Mr. Cooper would fling his arms around me for breaking the silence. "Why, yes, Lizzie!" he said loudly. "That's very kind of you."

"Won't be nothing much, but I reckon something's better than nothing."

"Not a soul around here's going to deny that."

I brought a chair out for Mr. Cooper to sit on, then headed into the kitchen. I'd decided to make biscuits. Each time I made them, the smell of the flour and buttermilk reminded me of the first time I'd tried. I was eight and Mama was sick with a cold. Daddy loved biscuits with supper, so I was determined to make them for him. I mixed all the ingredients together and stirred. And stirred. And stirred. They seemed a tad too wet and sticky so I added more flour. After a few more stirs, and some kneading, I cut them out and put them in to bake. It felt like years passed before they were ready, but when they were, I placed them in Mama's prettiest basket lined with a blue-and-white-checkered cloth.

They looked like Mama's—golden brown with a shiny butter top. Daddy grabbed one and bit. The biscuit bit back. It was hard as a rock. They all were. You could've hammered nails with them.

Mama let me practice a lot after that, and I'd gotten

much better at biscuits over the last four years. Now I was careful not to overmix or add so much flour. They usually came out like Mama's. Sometimes better.

Mr. Cooper had just finished his third biscuit with Mrs. Martin's pear preserves when Mrs. Sawyer came huffing around the side of the house. True to her word, both Sheriff Dawson and Dr. Heimler were tagging along behind her.

Dr. Heimler came onto the porch and narrowed his eyes at me. "What's this Mrs. Sawyer's telling me about your mother, Lizzie? Because from what I'm hearing, she's far worse than you let on. Why didn't you come get me? I left a note on the door."

My stomach did a backflip inside me, and every inch of my body went tingly. To save my life I couldn't think what I was supposed to say. I glanced at Erin. She had *that* look. The same one she'd had at school the day after the Myra Robinson incident. The same one she always had anytime she was on the verge of making somebody pay— her nostrils flared at the sides, one corner of her mouth turned upward in a sneer. Well, I wasn't about to let her see how scared I was. They could cart me off and leave me for dead and I wouldn't give her the satisfaction of seeing one bead of sweat or one single tear coming out of me.

Dr. Heimler shifted his weight. "I'm guessing you don't have a proper answer for me, then." He walked past me and went up to Mama.

"Now you see, Doctor," said Mrs. Sawyer, wagging her finger at Mama. "I told you she was bad."

Erin still hadn't said a word. I reckon there wasn't any need. She'd already put all the ingredients for trouble into the pot and stirred it, now all she had to do was enjoy watching it boil over.

Dr. Heimler patted Mama's hand and talked softly to her, but he didn't get in her face the way Mr. Cooper had. He didn't do much else besides take her pulse and flash a little light in her eyes.

"Well?" said Mrs. Sawyer. "What's to be done?"

"I need to think it over," said Dr. Heimler. "I don't want to make her worse."

"What about the girl? It's unthinkable to leave her here with no father, a mother in that condition, and the bank about to take their house. She has to go somewhere. Sheriff Dawson, did you do as I asked and call over to Brightside? That's the only reasonable option."

The sheriff stepped forward and removed his hat. "Yes'm. They said they had room. But what if we were to—"

"Were to what? Leave her here to her own devices? I should think not!"

Sheriff Dawson stepped back and stared down at the ground. He was bigger than two Mrs. Sawyers put together and wearing a sheriff's badge, to boot, but the way he was acting you'd think he was neither sizable nor sheriff.

Dr. Heimler spoke up. "Why don't you keep an eye on Lizzie, Mrs. Sawyer? Just until I've examined Mrs. Hawkins's condition more thoroughly."

Mrs. Sawyer reeled at that. She put her hand over her heart like she might die of shock at the mention of such a thing. "I should think not, Doctor. Lizzie terrorized Erin quite enough in school. And you should've heard the way she was speaking to me before we came for you. No, sir. I simply could not tolerate such an ill-behaved child in my house." She turned to me and grabbed hold of my arm. "Get your things together, Elizabeth Hawkins. You can't stay with me, but you're not staying here, either. Not while I'm still breathing."

"But what about Mama?" I jerked away from her grip and started toward Mama.

She grabbed me again, this time by the back of my shirt, and spun me around. "Oh, no you don't. You get to packing whatever you're planning to take. Dr. Heimler will take care of your mama."

Dr. Heimler didn't say anything. He only nodded. I couldn't tell what he was thinking. I wanted to ask, but I was too afraid of the answer. An answer I couldn't change no matter how badly I wanted to.

Mrs. Sawyer marched me back to my room. On my way I peeked one last time into Mama's. I made sure to keep it spotless. Nothing was out of place. The bed was so precisely made it looked as though it'd never been slept in. Even the homemade feather mattress atop the store-bought cotton one had been fluffed and smoothed to perfection. Mama would've done it that way if she could, but she couldn't, so I did it for her.

My room wasn't so lucky. My bed remained unmade, a wrinkled pile of blanket and quilt, topped off with a crooked, crumpled pillow. Books and papers were scattered about the room while my bookcase stood empty. For some reason, I could keep the entire house spotless, except for my room.

Mrs. Sawyer clucked her tongue at the sight. "I was right. You most certainly cannot stay here and live in a mess like this."

She'd failed to notice that the rest of the house was perfectly clean. I dug through the mess, gathering the belongings I wanted to take, and pretended not to hear her. I wanted to pack up my entire room—walls, bed, and all—and take it with me. The trouble was in fitting it all into my suitcase. I finally settled on two changes of clothes, a blanket, the slingshot Ben had given me, and my journal. I stacked them into my suitcase, and Mrs. Sawyer escorted me outside.

"Can't I say good-bye to Mama?"

"Lord, no. We'll never get you away from her if you start all that. I think it's better for everyone if you just go on with the sheriff."

Better for everyone? Who was "everyone"? I was pretty

sure it wasn't Mama or me. I could feel my chin tensing. *Don't let them see you cry. Don't let them.* The words rolled through my head.

Sheriff Dawson helped me into the backseat of his car. He was about to close the door when Erin came running up behind him.

"Would you excuse us, please, Sheriff?" she asked.

The sheriff nodded and went to settle in the driver's seat.

For the first time since she'd come back, Erin spoke to me. "I'm sorry this is happening to you, Lizzie," she whispered. "But that's life. Only some people get what they want, and right now I'm one of those people."

Erin slammed the car door in my face before I had the chance to reply. She and Mrs. Sawyer turned to go inside—inside my house, to look down on my mama. My arms and legs ached to run and punch and fight, but I could only watch as our house shrank smaller and smaller and finally disappeared from view.

~ *Eighteen* ~

'Tis Perseverance That Prevails

Poor Mama. I'd failed her. I'd let Erin win. Wasn't any doubt about it now. My chin again began to tremble, and this time there wasn't any stopping it. Salty tears streamed down my cheeks. Sheriff Dawson glanced back at me through the rearview mirror.

"I hate doin' this to ya, Lizzie," he said. "If there was a soul alive to look after you, I wouldn't. But as things is, I just ain't got a choice."

I didn't say anything back. I wasn't about to tell him it was all right for him to be dropping me off with strangers and leaving my mama alone with a doctor who'd send her off to heaven-knows-where. It wasn't all right. But since he was a nice man in all other respects, I didn't want to hurt his feelings either. I'd known even before he said it that he didn't *really* want to take me away. He just didn't know how to stand up to certain people. "Certain people" being Mrs. Sawyer.

I couldn't bear watching Sheriff Dawson's big eyes

looking back at me, so I opened my suitcase and pulled out my journal. The car bounced through a hole and the cover fell open. This time I didn't look away from that first entry. I read.

March 30, 1932

It was cold this morning—too cold for late March. Still, I jumped up just the same as always, and ran into the kitchen expecting to hear: Lizzie, I'm not going to tell you one more time to quit running through this house. *But Mama didn't say it. Instead, I found her slumped over the kitchen table, her head in her hands.*

"What's wrong, Mama?" I asked, patting her jerking back.

Her soft sniffles erupted into sobs. She stood without looking at me, staggered onto the back porch, and collapsed into the rocker.

A wrinkled note lay on the table, wet with Mama's tears. I picked it up and read the familiar handwriting flowing across the page:

Dearest Rose,
    Please understand. I can't bear to live like this—watching us all sink further and further into a hole. I feel so helpless. I can't

eat. I can't sleep. And I can't stop it by
staying.

I love you both. I'm terribly sorry, but I
have to go.

Give this to Lizzie for me.

Love always,
Will

*I looked around for the "this" Mama was
supposed to give me. It had fallen into a golden
pile beneath Mama's chair. The locket.*

*For the first time in more than a year, I looked
inside it. The pictures of Grandmother and
Grandfather had been replaced with pictures of
Daddy and me. I put the locket around my neck,
then I folded the note and put it in my dresser.*

*As I copied the note into this journal, I couldn't
help but wonder where Daddy's gone, and when
he'll come home. I guess there's no way to know.
Why doesn't he tell us? Is he afraid Mama will take
me and try to follow him? Is he afraid she'll try
to make him come home? I hope he writes soon. I
can't stand not knowing.*

On days after that, whenever I felt unsure Daddy would
come home, I'd pull that note from my dresser and read it
over. He hadn't said he was never coming back. Just that

he couldn't stop the bad by staying. I kept telling myself he'd be back. Lying to myself. Gripping on to hope with all that I had. But, like a block of ice left in the scorching summer sun, melting slowly at first and then faster and faster, my hope began to shrink smaller and smaller. The smaller it shrank, the faster it disappeared. Now hope evaporated. My lungs froze, refusing to inhale ever again.

I slammed the journal shut and shoved it back into my suitcase, trying to forget the memories of that day and the foolishness of my hope.

The words Mama had murmured that late afternoon on the porch played over and over in my mind: *Down for hair, just like your father.* Eventually those words faded to only four: *Just like your father. Just like your father.*

Mama knew. She'd always known. I was like Daddy. But I wanted to be, didn't I?

Mama's face appeared. Not the face she now possessed, but the face she'd once had—a face full of life and smiles. A face full of care and grace. The gripping in my lungs loosened and I inhaled. There was a chance Mama could still be that person. If Daddy had never gone, neither would she. Daddy had failed her. He'd left when she needed him to fight harder than he'd ever dreamed he'd have to.

Well, I wouldn't fail her. I wouldn't leave her. I'd fight. For her.

Then I knew, more surely than I'd ever known anything before, I didn't want to be like Daddy. I wanted to be better.

I had to get away from the sheriff. Escape. I wasn't about to end up in some orphanage. Nope. Not me. Besides, what bright side could any ol' orphanage possibly have?

I wiped the tears away from my face. The car jolted through another big pothole, and then, like a miraculous gift from God, I got an idea. A darned good idea. Mama! I grabbed my stomach and went to moaning and groaning.

"Lizzie, you all right back there?" Sheriff Dawson slowed the car a bit.

"Ugh," I groaned. I lay over in the seat. "I don't feel so good."

The car slowed a bit more, and the sheriff edged toward the side of the road. "What's wrong? You need me to pull over?"

I didn't reply. I wiggled and squirmed.

"Lizzie, I need you to tell me right now if you're gonna be sick." Sheriff Dawson gagged and took a deep breath. "I ain't so good at cleaning stuff like that up."

I puffed my cheeks with air like I was holding something down.

"I'm pullin' over right now. You're gonna have to get out and do that."

I looked up at him and nodded. His face had gone pale and he was taking more deep breaths than he should have been. He unbuttoned the top button of his shirt and fanned his face with his hat.

As soon as we stopped, he ran around and opened my

door. I grabbed my suitcase before I jumped out, but he didn't notice. He was too busy gagging and heaving and finding the nearest bush. And, my Lord, the noises that came from him once he found that bush.

I don't know when he finally realized I was missing. I was too far gone to care, running like mad through the woods away from his car. Running toward home.

~ Nineteen ~

A True Friend Is Known in the Day of Adversity

I ran till I thought I really *was* gonna be sick. I stopped long enough to give my legs a break from the beating my suitcase was giving them. I'd formed a plan while I was running, and I had to believe it would work. I pulled out my slingshot and studied it. Ben had never failed me, though I'd let him down more times than I could count. I prayed he'd let me make up for those failures.

Back in Bittersweet, I headed straight for Ben's. I jogged faster and faster. Then I started to run. I didn't have much time. I might already be too late.

Air heaved in and out of my lungs, and my shoes slapped hard against the dry ground. Mailboxes, houses, trees, they all streaked past in blurs, a mottle of colors and shapes. Then Ben's house appeared. The chickens scattered as I entered the yard. My head bobbed as I slowed my stride, causing the house to appear as if it were jumping for joy to see me. I felt the same.

I bounded up the front steps two by two, let my

suitcase drop to the porch with a bang, and jerked open the screen door. It creaked loudly in protest. I was gasping, trying to catch my breath, but fear didn't seem to care. It wrapped cold, strangling fingers around my neck and whispered ever so calmly that I was kidding myself. There was a good chance that Ben and his mother had already gone. And after our fight two days back, there was also a mighty good chance that Ben wouldn't want to see me even if they hadn't.

I looked at the darkened windows and listened for any sound of remaining life coming from inside. Nothing. I closed my eyes and gripped my slingshot, taking in deep breaths of the familiar scents around me—the warm wood of the house, the clean Christmasy scent of the pines, the sweetness of Mrs. Butler's gardenias. I raised my hand and knocked my usual *tap-t-t-tap*. The wooden door was rough and splintery against my knuckles. Painful silence drifted through the air. I squeezed my slingshot and tried once more, for myself. Not in Daddy's *tap-t-t-tap* but in a new knock, a knock only I could knock.

For a moment I thought I heard the faint popping of Ben's slingshot. Then the sound faded . . . and the door opened.

Ben stood in front of me. He studied me for a second with a question in his eyes, but he didn't ask it. There was no smile, no hint that he was happy to see me. I brushed the sweat off my face with my forearm and wiped it on my shirt. For once, I was unsure of what to say. I might as well have been a newborn, not able to talk, not able to say how I felt. It felt like I was seeing him for the first time. But if I was, I could start over. I could be the friend he needed instead of being the friend he was stuck with. I could care about him like I always should've, but never did.

Then, just like that, words came rushing back, and I knew what to say. Words I should've said a long time ago. "Are you all right?"

"You want the truth?" he asked.

I nodded, even though I knew the truth. I'd always known; I'd just been too concerned with myself to care.

Ben stepped out onto the porch and closed the door behind him. "I know I ain't perfect, and I don't pretend to be. But sometimes it seems like no matter how hard I try, things just don't go right." He studied his slingshot and sighed; then he looked back at me holding mine. "You look like you know what I'm talkin' about." He jerked his head toward my suitcase. "What's that for?"

"Sheriff Dawson came to take me over to the orphanage, but I got away."

Ben's mouth dropped open. "You did what? Ain't he lookin' for you?"

"I'm sure he is, but I had to come here first . . . to see about you . . . and to ask you something. I wasn't there when you needed me, Ben, and I'm sorry. But I want to be here for you now, if you'll let me."

Ben put his arm around my shoulders and squeezed

me. "You are my best friend, Lizzie, even if you aren't much of one sometimes."

I wanted to snort and stomp and say something smart, but I didn't. Because he was right. "You don't want to leave, do you?"

"No way in heck do I want to leave, but like I tried to tell you the other day, there ain't a whole lot I can do about it. I wish I had another chance to figure out some way we could stay. But I reckon I'm not like you, always figurin' how to get my own way. When Pa got sick, I tried to help him, but I couldn't, and when he died I figured it was best to just buck up and take what life dealt me."

"Well, what if I told you I've been figuring again? And what if my plan will help us help each other? Isn't that what being friends is all about?"

Ben scrunched his eyebrows, then let out a long sigh. "I ain't so sure I want to hear it, but I reckon it won't kill me to listen to you one more time."

"Wise decision," I said. Then I told Ben about my job, the mess I was in, and my plan—a plan that'd give us all a second chance.

Ben's eyes widened as I spilled it all out in one long breath. He smiled, then grabbed my hand and pulled me inside to find Mrs. Butler. We found her standing at the kitchen table boxing up some canned goods. Two closed suitcases sat against the wall. I figured they were already filled. Mrs. Butler looked up with a start, but Ben didn't wait for her to ask; he blurted out everything even faster than I had.

Mrs. Butler stared at us for a second like we'd gone off our rockers; then she began to smile too.

Ben walked over and squished up close to her. "Please, Ma," he whispered. "We can try."

Mrs. Butler laughed. "Oh, we can try all right. The thing that worries me is how I'm gonna keep you two out of trouble."

Ben threw his arms around his mother, and if I hadn't been coming at her from the other side, he'd have knocked her flat to the floor.

Mrs. Butler pried our arms away. "All right, both of you, let me go. You're suffocating the life out of me."

"Would you both mind coming home with me now?" I asked. "I don't want to go alone."

Ben looked at me and nodded, and Mrs. Butler took my hand. She squeezed it. "Of course we'll come with you. Look there." She pointed to the suitcases. "We're already packed and ready to go."

Chills ran up and down my limbs just thinking about having to face those people hovering around Mama alone. But I knew one thing for certain—I wouldn't have to. "You know," I said, "needing people isn't half as bad as I thought it'd be."

Mrs. Butler sighed. "No, honey, it's not needin' people that's so bad, it's needin' people when there's not a soul around that's the worst." She grabbed me and squeezed me tight. She leaned over and looked me square in the eyes, the way Mama used to when she was saying something important. "I want you to know that I'm going to do everything I can to help your mama. I should've done it two months ago; I just wasn't sure Rose wanted me there, but I was wrong. She needed me whether she wanted me or not."

In that moment I knew Mrs. Butler had forgiven Mama, and I wasn't sure she'd ever been angry, just sad—sad about losing Mr. Butler, sad about losing Mama, sad that she was alone when she needed someone the most, sad she hadn't taken the chance to be there for Mama. And in that very same moment, I was sad. Sad that I'd waited so long to reach out to the people that I loved, people who'd been there the whole time waiting to reach out to me. Mrs. Butler hadn't had that, but I had—Mr. Hinkle, Ben, Mrs. Butler, even Miss Jones—and I hadn't treated it like the blessing it was. I'd nearly thrown it away, but I never would again. Of that I *was* sure.

Mrs. Butler and Ben grabbed their suitcases and the three of us rushed out the door, headed home to help Mama. If she was still in the state she'd been in earlier, the doctor and the others would be having a mighty hard time convincing her to leave that back-porch rocker. Not all folks agree, but I think stubbornness can be a right good quality to have sometimes.

As we raced down the road, I glanced up. Puffy white clouds meandered across a brilliant blue sky. I smiled. If my emotions had a color, that was it—fresh, stainless white slowly covering a deep, sad blue.

Half a mile later, huffing and puffing, we rounded the side of the house. Just as I'd figured, Mama wasn't budging. Mrs. Sawyer was pulling Mama's right hand while Dr. Heimler was pressing against her back, trying to get her to stand. We walked onto the porch and put down our suitcases. It showed what I wanted to say: we were staying. Mama's visitors—Mrs. Sawyer, Erin, Dr. Heimler, Mr. Cooper, and even the sheriff, who must've overcome his sickness at last—stared at us.

Mrs. Sawyer stared at Mrs. Butler, her eyes fluttering faster than a butterfly's wings. From the look of her, I figured her inner wheels were turning, trying to figure out exactly who Mrs. Butler was and what she was doing there.

Erin glared at Ben and folded her arms across her chest. "Should've known," she said. Mrs. Butler looked confused and stared down at Ben for an answer.

"Me and Ma's just tryin' to help, that's all," Ben said.

Erin huffed. Her face puckered up in that all-too-familiar lemon look.

Dr. Heimler and the sheriff hadn't seemed to notice any of the other happenings around 'em. They were too all-fired busy staring at me. Sheriff Dawson wagged his finger at me and shook his head. Mr. Cooper just stood there looking as confused as a cow standing in front of a new gate. He didn't know whether to go or stay.

Mrs. Butler broke the silence. She slowly walked over to Mama and took her hand. "Rose," she whispered. "Rose. It's me, Louise. Me and Ben have come to stay with you, if that's all right. We seem to be having a pretty rough go of it." For only the second time since Daddy had left, Mama turned her head toward a voice. Mrs. Butler patted her hand in response. "We're gonna stay with you, Rose. With you and Lizzie."

Dr. Heimler edged over to Mrs. Butler and whispered something in her ear. Mrs. Butler nodded. She placed her hand under Mama's arm and said, "I'm gonna help you inside now. Dr. Heimler needs to take a look at you, and you can come back out when he's finished. He wants to help you."

Dr. Heimler put his hand under Mama's other arm and they helped her to her feet.

The doctor said to me as he passed, "Stay here. I'll be back."

With only Mr. Cooper, Sheriff Dawson, and her mother now present, Erin took the opportunity to lash out at Ben. "I knew it," she said, her voice sharp and stinging. "You never were my friend. You were just mad at her." She pointed at me. "Well, guess what. I wasn't your friend either. I just wanted you to think I was."

Ben stepped close to Erin. "I don't believe you." His

voice was soft and steady. "You wanted me to be your friend. I wanted to be yours. Still do. But you gotta stop all this battlin' between you and Lizzie." Ben turned around and looked at me. He smiled. "Heck, Erin, I'm even nice to rattlesnakes, and some folks around here don't think that's too smart. But I figure as long as I know where the snake stands, and it knows where I stand, we'll get along all right. I won't hurt it, but it's got to trust me enough not to hurt me either. Understand?"

Erin didn't stop long enough to hear anything Ben was saying. "I understand you think you can have it both ways. You think you can march around here being friends with me and with Miss Know-It-All. Well, let me be the first to tell you, that isn't gonna happen."

Mrs. Sawyer stepped forward and put her arm around Erin's shoulders. Erin pulled away. She scowled at Ben and sulked over to the railing on the far side of the porch. Ben shook his head and walked back over to me. Mr. Cooper and the sheriff tried their darndest to pretend they weren't standing smack in the middle of an argument. Well, they should've thought about that before they butted their noses into my business.

An early evening breeze began to blow. It cooled the porch after the heat of the day. The pond and the woods beyond it grew shadowy in the twilight. Ben and I sat down on the top step of the porch and I closed my eyes. I wondered what Dr. Heimler was talking to Mrs. Butler about, and if he'd examined Mama.

I didn't have to wait long to find out. The back door creaked open, breaking the quiet. The doctor and Mrs. Butler came back onto the porch.

"Where's Mama?" I asked, jumping up from the step.

Mrs. Butler came over to me. "She's sitting in her chair, honey." She turned and nodded at Dr. Heimler.

He cleared his throat. "As we all can see," he said, motioning toward the sky, "it's getting rather late. Mrs. Hawkins is beginning to tire, so I suggest we resume this discussion in the morning."

Mrs. Sawyer stomped forward. "You can't be serious, Doctor. You're going to leave them like this?"

The doctor nodded. "Frankly, I fail to see the problem, Mrs. Sawyer. Mrs. Butler will be here with Lizzie, and she's perfectly capable of watching over everything. I think the best thing for all of us is to get a good night's rest and sort this out first thing in the morning."

"Well, I must tell you, I do not agree."

Dr. Heimler rubbed his eyes with his fingers. "You don't have to agree with me, but you spoke to me of your concern for Mrs. Hawkins several weeks back, and now that her care is in my hands, I'm trying my best to do right by her. It does her no good to be up and out of her usual routine. My goal, Mrs. Sawyer, is to make her better, not worse. So, everyone"—he motioned toward the porch steps—"if we would all be so kind as to leave, I'm sure Lizzie and Mrs. Butler have things to attend to. We'll all meet back here at nine in the morning."

The sheriff and Mr. Cooper tipped their hats to Mrs. Butler as they passed. I reckoned they were more than ready to leave. They'd already witnessed more than they'd bargained for. Erin refused to look at either me or Ben.

Mrs. Sawyer pushed past the doctor on her way to the steps. "I never would've believed you'd let your emotions get the better of you, Dr. Heimler."

The doctor didn't respond. He tipped his hat to us and followed Mrs. Sawyer and Erin down the steps. As they all rounded the corner, the feeling of freedom filled me. But I knew there was a big chance that feeling would get knocked out of me at nine o'clock in the morning. I had to think of something else to keep us all together. To keep us all home.

The three of us walked inside to check on Mama. She was sitting in her chair, beginning to nod off. Mrs. Butler looked at me. "Ben and I will ready one of the spare rooms; you tend to your mama." She walked out to her new room, and Ben followed her.

Mama's book was hanging on for dear life at the edge of her lap. I picked it up and gently shook her. "Come on. Time for bed."

She let me lead her to her room and help her into her nightgown. "We're gonna be just fine, Mama. I promise. Don't you worry about anything."

As I brushed and braided her hair, I wondered if now she'd start to get better. She'd recognized Mrs. Butler out on the porch. I'd seen it. Surely Dr. Heimler had too. I felt like this night was Dr. Heimler's way of giving us a chance to prove we could make it work. And if we could prove it, then he'd work with us, not against us. He wasn't gonna be buffaloed by Mrs. Sawyer the way the sheriff had, and I respected him for it.

I helped Mama into bed and pulled the covers up over her. To me, she looked better already. I gripped my locket as I stood over her, praying for God to send me a sign—any sign—as to how to keep the house away from the bank. Mama would get better with all of us together at home. I knew it. I rubbed at the rough lines of my locket's engraving and pictured the two faces inside. For the first time since Daddy had gone, God must've heard my prayers, because like I was seeing a flash of lightning cutting through the darkness, I knew exactly what I had to do.

~ Twenty ~

The Greatest Conqueror
Is He Who Conquers Himself

I jumped out of bed at the crack of dawn. Mr. Hinkle opened up at seven sharp, and I'd be waiting when he did. I put on my church dress just for the occasion. You're supposed to dress nicely for business dealings, and business dealings were what I'd be having most of the morning— first with Mr. Hinkle and then with some other not-so-nice people after that. When I crossed the hall to get Mama, I could smell coffee brewing in the kitchen. If Mrs. Butler had been an early bird before she moved in, she'd be one after. Pigs would fly before she'd change her schedule.

Mama was already sitting up on the side of her bed. She looked up at me. "Morning, Mama. Mrs. Butler's got your coffee brewing. Are you ready to get dressed?"

No reply. Oh, well, wasn't anything new.

I went over to her dresses and pulled out the pink floral with the lace collar and white buttons, the same one I'd dressed her in nearly a month earlier—the last day she'd actually spoken to me. But unlike the last time I'd put it on her, this time I helped her slip on her silk stockings, making sure the seam down the back was perfectly straight, and brushed her hair back into a neat bun at the base of her neck. I knew we'd be having visitors for the second day in a row, and I wanted to be sure Mama looked proper for them. She'd want that too.

Mrs. Butler looked up from the grits on the cookstove when we came in. "Oh, Rose," she said as she clasped her hands together. "You look beautiful today." Mrs. Butler smiled at me; then she turned and spooned some grits into a bowl for Mama. I poured the coffee and topped it off with some milk. It was one of the few times since Daddy had left that Mama had eaten breakfast at the kitchen table. The sight of her sitting there in her pink dress with her smooth bun filled me with hope.

"Where's Ben?" I asked Mrs. Butler.

"Oh, he's already gone over to Mr. Reed's, dear. Sometimes I believe that boy would live there if I'd let him." She laughed. "I never would've thought it. Not in a thousand years." She shook her head and walked back over to the stove to take the biscuits from the oven.

"I need to run over to Hinkle's this morning, if that's all right," I said. "I've got something I need to do before all the vultures come back."

Mrs. Butler turned around to face me. She was grinning but trying to hide it. I could tell. "Now, Lizzie, they're not vultures. They're just trying to help, that's all."

"Yeah," I said. "Help us right out of our house."

"I'm sure that's not what they want." She sat down across from Mama and took a sip of coffee. "Not all of them, anyway." She winked, and I knew she was talking about Erin and Mrs. Sawyer. "Now, hadn't you best get on with what you need to get done? I'll take care of your mama till you get back. Ben's supposed to come home early and help me get the rest of our belongings—the ones we're allowed to take."

"Yes, ma'am. Thank you. For everything."

"Thank you, too."

I nodded, then kissed Mama's cheek. "Be back," I said, and I was out the door, jogging down toward Hinkle's.

The sun was up above the tree line now, and the birds were chirping and singing like it was the end of days. There wasn't a cloud to be seen, and when I finally reached Hinkle's, the glass door gleamed in the morning light. I pushed it open, and the bell clanked above my head. I said a quick prayer that my plan would work. Whether it did or not, I owed it to Mama and to Ben to try.

Mr. Hinkle looked up from the figures inside his notebook. "Mighty early this mornin', Miss Lizzie. You decide you love working here so much you just gotta be around for opening too?" He looked back down at his notebook and scribbled something.

"Mr. Hinkle, can I talk to you about something?" He closed his notebook and looked at me. At least I had his attention. "I'll start at the beginning." He already knew about Daddy—that was common knowledge around town, but that was just about all he knew. In close to one breath I spilled out the whole rest of the story—the parts about Erin, and the bank, and the orphanage and Mama. The whole ugly truth.

Mr. Hinkle's eyes widened as I spoke. The wider they got, the less they twinkled. "Why didn't you tell me all this a long time ago?"

"I didn't want to let Daddy down. He'd want me to take care of things by myself. I figured it wouldn't count if I got help."

"Oh, Lizzie, I'm sure if your daddy could see you now, he'd be prouder than he ever thought he could be."

There'd been a time when I thought I'd burst into a million pieces if I heard my daddy was proud of me, but now that I'd heard it, it didn't matter anymore. *I* was proud of me, and right now that felt better than a mountain of Goo Goo Clusters waiting for me on Christmas morning.

"So, here's what I wanted to ask you." I reached up and gripped my locket. I rubbed it for the last time, then took it off and placed it on the counter in front of him. I somehow felt lighter with it off. "Are you still interested in buying this?"

Mr. Hinkle picked up the locket and studied it, the corners of his eyes crinkled even more than usual. He didn't say anything. He didn't even grunt. He just kept looking at the locket, then me, then the locket. Finally he spoke. "You sure, Lizzie? You seemed pretty intent on keeping it a while back. Its sale would be final, you know. Won't be any taking it away from Mrs. Hinkle once she's wearing it."

"Yes, sir. I understand. How much do you think it's worth?"

He rubbed his chin for a few seconds. "I figure around ten dollars."

"So that's your best offer?" I crossed my fingers, and toes, for good measure. If he hadn't been looking me square in the face, I'd have crossed my eyes. Ten dollars was more than I'd dreamed.

"It is. What do you say?"

I could've leapt square over the counter and flung my arms around him, but I thought better of it. He was my boss now, after all. I had to try to act professional. "Yes, sir," I said. "I'll take it."

I removed the faded pictures of me and Daddy from the locket and placed them in my left pocket. Then I carefully folded the ten dollars and put them in my right.

Mr. Hinkle watched me without saying a word, as though he thought I shouldn't *really* be selling my locket.

"May I ask for one more thing?" I said.

"Go ahead and ask, but I can't promise you anything. You've near cleared me out this morning, and we still got the rest of the day to go."

"It won't cost you anything," I said. "I was wondering if you had any old boxes I could use to make a sign to hang in your window."

"Sure do. I have plenty of old boxes, but what in the world do you need to make a sign for?"

"For more boarders."

"Boarders? You taking in boarders?"

"Yes, sir," I said. "Got the Butlers living with us already."

"Well, good for you. You best make that sign as pretty as possible. I hear the Martins are some tough competition for boarder seekers."

"Don't worry. I'm pretty sure Mrs. Martin's got all the people she can handle right now."

"Well, all righty, then. Be back in a jiffy with a box. You cut it to the size of your liking."

Before long I had my sign. I thought it looked pretty good. Not as good or colorful as Mr. Hinkle's signs or anything, but eye-catching in its own way. He showed me the best window to display it in.

I was taping the first corner to the glass when Mrs. Hinkle came scurrying through. She came to a sudden halt and stared at my sign. "Land sakes, look at that! Letting her trash up our front windows when I cleaned them just this morning. Injustice! That's what it is."

I looked over at Mr. Hinkle, expecting to see his usual twinkly eyes and slyly grinning lips, but they'd disappeared. His face was hard, his teeth clenched. He jammed his hand into his pocket, yanked out the locket, and marched over to Mrs. Hinkle. Not an inch from her face he hollered, "I've had enough! After forty-two years of your yammering on and on and on, I've had enough, I tell you!"

Mrs. Hinkle, for possibly the first time in her entire life, was stunned into silence. "Why, Herbert," she whispered.

"Don't you 'Why, Herbert' me. If I have to hear one more word, I'll fire you. Don't you dare think I won't." He jerked his thumb toward me. "I already got your replacement lined up." He snatched up her hand and plunked the locket into it. "There you are. That should keep you quiet for a while. Though why in this world Lizzie had to give it up to you is beyond me. There has to be a more deserving person out there." He closed her hand around the locket. "Injustice! That's what it is."

Mr. Hinkle stomped back to his counter, and Mrs. Hinkle slumped off into the back. I finished hanging my sign, making sure it was straight and checking that none of the words were hidden from view.

Mr. Hinkle's outburst had convinced me that there was some justice in the world. That outburst was exactly what Mrs. Hinkle deserved. I wasn't sure how long her pouting spell would last, but I thought if there was any justice for Mr. Hinkle, it'd last for the next forty-two years.

I turned back into our drive just before nine and rushed inside to check on Mama. Mrs. Butler had helped her out onto the back porch and was sitting beside her, cutting some squares for a new quilt.

"How is she?" I asked.

Mrs. Butler glanced over at Mama. "She's fine." She paused and then went on, "She'll be just fine." She went back to her cutting and I went inside to grab $10.90 from the emergency savings jar and $1.60 from the jar under my bed. I carefully folded the money together with the $10.00 from the locket and put it into my pocket.

I'd just finished combing my hair when a knock at the front door rattled through the air. Mrs. Butler must've heard too, because she'd already let the whole gaggle of 'em in by the time I made it to the front door.

"Good morning," she was saying as I came into the parlor. "I trust you all slept well."

All the men—Mr. Cooper, the sheriff, and Dr. Heimler—nodded and removed their hats. "Very well, thank you," they said. But not Mrs. Sawyer. Oh, no. She hadn't slept a wink worrying herself silly about us.

Mrs. Butler tried to be patient. "I'm terribly sorry to hear that, Mrs. Sawyer. May I get you some coffee?"

"That may do some good, if you don't mind."

"Not at all. Please make yourselves comfortable. Lizzie, will you help me?"

In the kitchen, I confronted Mrs. Butler about her overly nice ways. "You haven't got to be that friendly, you know. A pair of 'em aren't all that nice anyway."

She placed the sugar bowl onto a serving tray and said, "Don't you know you can catch more flies with honey than with vinegar?"

"No, ma'am, but it sure does sound like something

Mama would say." I took enough coffee cups from the cabinet to serve the men too.

Mrs. Butler stopped filling the creamer and looked at me. "You know, I do believe that's where I heard it."

We finished pouring the coffee and put it onto the tray with the cream and sugar. We placed it on the table in front of the sofa and let the guests serve themselves. Dr. Heimler and Erin were the only ones who didn't take any.

"How is your mama this morning, Lizzie?" he asked. "Do you mind if I take a look at her?"

"She's fine, sir. She's out on the back porch."

"Shall we, then?"

We all herded out to the porch and converged around Mama. Erin's eyes darted back and forth between Mama and the doctor. He bent and gently held Mama's wrist, feeling her pulse. He nodded and placed her hand back on her book.

"Well, Dr. Heimler, what do you think?" Mrs. Butler whispered, her voice tight. She took a deep breath and laid her hand across her chest.

The doctor stepped over to me, the lines across his forehead softer than they'd been the day before. "I understand that you want to take care of your mama, Lizzie, but how are you going to manage that with no place to live?"

"Oh, we'll have a place to live, all right, and it'll be here. I'll pay Mr. Cooper his money right this minute, and we'll pay him every month from here on. Don't you doubt it."

Mrs. Sawyer huffed. "And where exactly are you getting the money? It's certainly not falling from the sky."

"No, ma'am, it's not. It's coming straight out of my pocket." I pulled the $22.50 from my dress pocket and marched the neatly folded money right over to Mr. Cooper. "Here you go," I said. "Go on and count it. It's all there."

Mr. Cooper did as I instructed. After he finished counting, he looked up, his jaw hanging lower than a hound dog's ears. "I'll be doggoned," he said. "It's all here." He tipped his hat at me. "Pleasure doin' business with you, Miss Lizzie. I hope everything works out for you. Now, I do believe my job here is done. I'll just be going."

Mrs. Sawyer gasped. "Don't you have any interest, Mr. Cooper, in exactly where that money came from?"

Erin gaped at the money being shoved into Mr. Cooper's pocket. "How in the world did *you* get that much money? Mr. Hinkle isn't paying you that much. You stole it, didn't you?"

Mr. Cooper stared down at me, awaiting my explanation. Well, he'd hear it. They'd all hear it good.

"I most certainly did not steal it. I sold my locket to Mr. Hinkle, took some money from Mama and Daddy's savings jar, and worked for the rest myself. Go ask Mr. Hinkle if you don't believe me. He'll tell you real quick I'm not lying."

Mr. Cooper patted my shoulder. "Good enough for me." He wheeled around and was gone before anyone else could question me.

I looked at Erin. The color had drained from her face. She looked as if she was about to bust out crying, her nostrils flared, her chin quivering.

"Listen, Lizzie," said Sheriff Dawson in a voice so soft it was as if he was scared of it. "You make it all sound good, but I ain't so sure it'll work."

"I've got one thing to say," I yelled, "and I'm only gonna say it once! I'm sick to death of you telling me what'll work and what won't! Mama needs me, that's all I know. And I need her. Nobody can help her but me; I know it deep inside me. I will not leave her like Daddy did. I'm staying. I'm trying. There's no law against trying, is there?"

There. I'd said it. They could love it or hate it. Their choice.

Dr. Heimler placed a hand on my shoulder. "There's no law against trying, but you must understand that chances are you won't get her back. Still, I do believe she stands a much higher chance of recovery with you here. Without you, she'll continue to shut out the world until eventually she'll be lost for good. I'd like to help you try, if you'll let me." He knelt down and looked straight into my eyes. "You may not think she notices your presence, but I promise she knows when you're here and when you're not."

A flood of emotion washed over me. I'd known all along. Every time I talked to Mama, waved to her, brought her a meal, I knew she felt me there even if she didn't show it. Now I had to do something for Mama that Dr. Heimler never could—prove to her I'd stay, even if I lost my job, my pride, my most valuable possession. No matter what, I'd always stay.

"I promise, Mama," I whispered. "I'm not leaving you. Ever."

Then it happened. Erin lost it. She lurched at Mrs. Sawyer and clutched her mother's dress, tears streaming down her red cheeks. "Please, do something! It's not fair. You can't let her stay. You can't! I'll never be good enough with her in my way."

Mrs. Sawyer grabbed ahold of Erin and pulled her close. "What in heaven's name has gotten into you? Good enough for what?" For the first time since I'd known her, Mrs. Sawyer finally looked embarrassed.

Erin pushed away from Mrs. Sawyer's grasp. "What do you care?" she shouted. "You don't. You only wanted me because you couldn't have your own baby, didn't you? Well, I'm not yours, and I never will be, so stop fooling yourself. One day I'll be somebody. I'll be somebody so important, my real mother won't be able to ignore me anymore. Then she'll be sorry she ever left me. But I'm already sorry. Sorry I have to be stuck with you."

The doctor and the sheriff stood there, their eyes darting back and forth from each other to Erin and her mother. I didn't know what they were thinking, but I knew what I was: *It was true. Erin was adopted.* The thought of it rolled over and over again in my mind, and in that moment I almost felt sorry for her. Almost. Until she came barging at me.

"It's not fair! You always get everything you want. And I'm not going to let it happen this time."

"I don't get everything I want. If I did, my daddy would be standing here right now. But he isn't, and I'm not sure he ever will be again." The words spilled out. The truth spilled out.

"But you still have your mother." Tears rolled down her cheeks and dripped onto the porch floor. "I've never even seen mine. Do you know what that's like? She gave me up before I could even know her. She didn't *want* to know *me*. I figure, if you can't trust your own mother, you can't trust anybody."

Mrs. Sawyer leaned over to Erin. "What about me?" she whispered. "You don't trust me?"

Erin's look could've burned a hole through steel. "I've already trusted somebody like you. She said I belonged to her. She said she loved me." Erin wiped the tears from her cheeks. "Well, not long after that, the doctor told her she was gonna have a baby of her own—a baby who truly did belong to her. And where did I end up? Right back where I'd started. The orphanage. Why should I think you're any different? Why should I trust you? Nobody *really* wants an orphan, do they?"

Mrs. Sawyer spoke, her voice almost a whisper. "If we didn't want you, then why did we move over here from Georgia to protect you? We were trying to give you a fresh start, where no one knew; where none of the kids would tease you or laugh at you; where you could be normal."

"Normal?" Erin's voice sliced through the heavy air. "Just go on and say it, why don't you? You're ashamed for people to know you had to go off and adopt a kid instead of having one of your own. That's the real reason we moved, and don't you try and say any different. Those kids couldn't have hurt me. I can take care of myself. I don't need you, or anybody else, moving me here or anywhere, you understand me?"

Mrs. Sawyer looked as crushed as stalks of sorghum cane after milling. She steadied herself against the porch railing. After a few seconds, she found her voice. "I have some things that need my immediate attention. If you'll all excuse me."

Mrs. Sawyer tried to put her arm around Erin's shoulder, but Erin dodged her. She stomped off the porch and around the house. Mrs. Sawyer followed, trying to keep up. I looked over at Mama and I knew that even in the state she was in, she loved me. She would never give me up. That, I had never doubted. And I loved her right back, and I wasn't about to give her up either. Erin had never known that.

Without thinking twice, I took off after Erin. "Wait!" I shouted when I reached the drive. Mrs. Sawyer turned to face me. Erin didn't.

"Erin, you were right. I'm sorry. I should've just stayed out of the essay contest. It's true. I do want to win everything, and it isn't fair. If I had it to do over, I wouldn't sign up in the first place."

She turned. I tried to read her face, but there was nothing to read. Her lips were pulled into a hard, thin line, her eyes blank. "I figured you'd get desperate enough to apologize, but I've known you long enough to know you don't apologize for anything."

I was saying I was sorry, and I truly was, and she was gonna hear me whether she wanted to or not. "Maybe the old Lizzie didn't apologize, but the new one does."

Erin laughed, her long braids swaying like snakes about to strike. "The new Lizzie? But the old Lizzie was supposed to be perfect."

She started to go. I grabbed her hand to stop her. Our eyes locked. Her pupils grew and shrank as shadows danced across the drive. She didn't drop my hand. "You listen to me, Erin. I don't care if you believe me or not, and I'm not about to stand around here all day trying to convince you, but I *am* sorry. If you're trying to make me scared of you, you're wasting your time. I'm not scared—not anymore. You don't have to be either. If you want to trust someone, you can trust Ben. He won't let you down. I know it's hard to trust people, but I guess we have to try, or else we'll end up alone. Is that what you want?" What I'd said was truth. Love-it-or-hate-it truth.

Erin's face was all pinched up like she was about to cry again. She let go of me. "Ben?" Her voice cracked. "How can I trust Ben? He's moved into your house." She dropped my hand and walked away. I watched her until she disappeared from view.

Though I couldn't see her, I knew—love it or hate it, she believed me. Whether she forgave me was her decision, her business. I'd done what I could to help her, even though she'd done all she could to hurt me.

I jogged back to Mama filled with a new pride. I'd admitted a wrong to a person who, at this moment, was determined to be a pure enemy, and yet I'd never felt so strong. So . . . free.

Dr. Heimler looked at me and smiled. "Don't you think you should start posting some signs asking for a few more boarders? I really don't think two is going to be much help."

"Done," I said. "Already got one hanging at Hinkle's."

"Good. I suppose we need to have a long talk about your mama. See where we stand."

Sheriff Dawson cleared his throat to get my attention. "Before I go," he said as he reached for my arm, "I'd like a word with you in private."

Dr. Heimler shrugged. He took Mama's hand and led her carefully toward the door. She went willingly. Mrs. Butler went inside to ready Mama's chair.

The sheriff squeezed in close to me and bent down to my ear. "I'm real glad you think you've found a way to stay with your mama and all, but I don't much appreciate you pullin' that trick on me yesterday. Nobody's gonna take me seriously if I can't even get . . ." His voice trailed off, and he swiped his hand across his shiny forehead. "I mean, what are folks gonna think when they find out how you got away? You got to promise me something."

I glanced over at Dr. Heimler. He was only halfway to the door.

"Promise what?" I whispered back.

Sheriff Dawson edged in closer. "Promise me you won't ever say one word about exactly *how* you got away from me. I don't care what tall tale you gotta come up with, as long as it don't make me look so stupid as the truth."

Pictures of big, burly Sheriff Dawson hovering over those bushes gagging like crazy flashed through my mind. My belly rolled in and out like waves of hay blowing in the breeze. My stomach muscles tightened to keep me from busting out laughing worse than I ever had. It'd been the funniest thing I'd seen since birth, but it gave me power. Power to barter. One thing was certain—Sheriff Dawson was terrified of someone finding out his weakness and of becoming the laughingstock of Bittersweet, and that terror far outweighed his fear of Mrs. Sawyer and his need to cart me off to Brightside Orphanage.

I looked him dead in the eyes. He winced. "I'll promise on one condition," I said.

"Shhh." He put his finger against his lips and pointed at the doctor.

I lowered my voice. "I promise I won't say anything as long as you don't come around here again trying to haul me off to the orphanage. All I want to do is stay here and help Mama. If you get your way, I get mine. Fair is fair. We got a deal?" I stuck out my hand.

He glanced around once more at the doctor. His back was turned to us now, but his shoulders were shaking rather suspiciously. The sheriff eyed him for a minute, then took my hand. "Deal."

I walked back over to Dr. Heimler and Mama as if nothing had happened. The sheriff cleared his throat and said to Dr. Heimler, "You didn't . . . uhhh . . . hear any of that, did you?"

The doctor stopped Mama and looked at the sheriff in perfectly acted confusion, a performance that would've made Douglas Fairbanks proud. "Hear what?"

"Oh, nothin'. Well, I need to be headin' on out; got lots of duties that need tendin' to."

Sheriff Dawson strutted like a rooster around the side of the house. When he finally started his car, all seriousness was shattered by the two of us, Dr. Heimler and me, laughing till we cried.

Ben had been right that day on the street. Dr. Heimler wasn't the type of doctor to go around abandoning folks in mental wards. He was the kind that truly cared, truly wanted to help. He'd proven it.

Like I said, people aren't always what they seem. Sometimes they seem worse than they are. Sometimes better. The trouble is you never can tell who is who. That was why, as far as Dr. Heimler went, I was going to trust him, because for Mama's sake, it was better to be safe than sorry.

~ *Twenty-One* ~

A Friend Is Not Known Till He Is Lost

Mid-June came fast, with less rain and more heat. June had always been my favorite month. I loved it for the long summer evenings: the fireflies, the crickets, the local whip-poor-will whistling its name at dusk. The evenings were peaceful and warm. They soothed away bits and pieces of the sadness I felt about Daddy not showing up on my birthday, but they couldn't heal me completely.

Over the next month, Ben and I continued to work—me at Hinkle's, him at Mr. Reed's. Erin dropped Ben quicker than a hot potato. She couldn't get over him moving in with us. If she happened to be in town at the same time we were, she'd turn around and hightail it the other way. And she didn't dare set a toenail in Hinkle's during my work hours anymore. Ben said he went over one afternoon after work and tried to talk to her, but she wouldn't even come to the door.

Around the last of June, a family by the name of Wilkins came to board with us—a couple in their mid-twenties along with their two-year-old daughter, a little girl with white-blond hair named Clara. They took my room and I moved in with Mama. They were kind—both to us and to each other—and they made me think of how me, Mama, and Daddy might've been when I was a baby.

Right after Daddy left, watching the Wilkinses would've deepened the cut of sadness inside me, but with Mama getting better, and Ben and Mrs. Butler around, the sadness seemed to be scarring over.

By Independence Day, we'd managed to keep the house paid up and the bank off our heels. When we weren't working or helping our mothers, Ben would give me slingshot lessons or take me over to Mr. Reed's, and when it was time for Bittersweet's yearly fireworks, I was invited to watch them with Mr. Reed and Ben. For the first time in our whole lives, Ben and I didn't watch the show from the curb in front of Powell's. Instead, we sat out on the grass in Mr. Reed's clean front yard. You could see everything from up on that hill. We all sat together watching the fireworks burst and sparkle over the town. Ziggy stayed right beside Ben the whole time, barking at every pop and boom like the world was on fire.

"Ziggy, you'd best hush up or I'm gonna put you inside," Mr. Reed scolded in between cigarette puffs.

Ziggy didn't hush. Mr. Reed didn't put him in.

I'd only been visiting Mr. Reed for about two weeks, but already he seemed a different person than what I'd cooked up in my mind. He wasn't scary or crazy, he'd been just plain ol' sad and lonely. He wasn't quite as sad or lonely anymore. I figured maybe his cut of sadness was scarring over, too.

Two weeks before school was set to start, Mr. Reed came down with a hacking cough. For over a week Ben and I listened to him.

"Let me get Dr. Heimler for you, Mr. Reed. Ain't no trouble," Ben said to him during one particularly bad fit.

"No, son, I don't need no doctor. It'll pass."

But it didn't pass. On Sunday morning, Ben and I went to check on him. He didn't answer the door. Ben looked at me, the skin under his pale brows reddening.

"Mr. Reed," he called. "You in there? It's Ben and Lizzie."

No answer.

"Mr. Reed?"

No answer.

From outside we could hear Ziggy running through the house, coming to Ben's voice. He whined and scratched at the door. Ben couldn't stand it. He stopped waiting on Mr. Reed and just barged right in. Ziggy's food and water bowls stood empty, and a bowl of untouched oatmeal sat on the table.

"Mr. Reed?" Ben called again. "It's me and Lizzie. You in here?"

"Let's go check in his room," I said. "Something's wrong."

We tiptoed back to Mr. Reed's room. He was there in

his bed, buried beneath a pile of quilts. Ben ran over to him and felt his forehead. "He's burning up. Go get Dr. Heimler, will ya? Hurry!"

I didn't think twice. I bolted out the door and down into town. I'd have to go through town and all the way past the Martins' to get to him. And even then, there was a chance he wouldn't be home.

"Please, God," I prayed aloud, my voice jumping as my feet pounded the ground. "Please, let the doctor be home."

I ran onto his front porch and was about to pound on the door when it flew open. "Mr. Reed" was all I could manage between gasps for air.

"Jump in the car," Dr. Heimler ordered. "I'll grab my things."

I did as I was told. By now, I'd have been glad to never have to ride in a car again. Riding in a sheriff's car and a doctor's car weren't my idea of joyrides. If you saw either one of those coming for you, you weren't having such a good go of it. Still, I had to admit, there was one good thing about Dr. Heimler's car: it went a lot faster than I could run, and in a few minutes, we were back at Mr. Reed's.

Ben had pulled a chair into the bedroom and was sitting beside Mr. Reed's bed. Ziggy was curled up on the floor at Ben's feet. He let out a long whine when we entered.

"He's bad off, Doctor," Ben said, his voice cracking. "I think it might be pneumonia. I can hear it rattlin'."

Dr. Heimler checked over Mr. Reed's frail body, listening here, feeling the pulse there. Finally he spoke. "You're right, Ben. Pneumonia." The doctor looked up at me. "Lizzie, you run on home and help your mother and Mrs. Butler. Ben will stay with me in case I need anything."

"Yes, sir." I did as I was told without argument, even though what I really wanted to do was stay with Ben. I knew how hard he'd take it if Mr. Reed passed away. A part of me thought it wasn't fair for God to let Mr. Reed die like this, just a year and a half since Ben had lost his pa.

Ben spent the next three days at Mr. Reed's with Dr. Heimler. After school each day and work each afternoon, I'd run home and get boxed suppers and take them up to Mr. Reed's. Dr. Heimler would clean his plate. Ben did good to eat five bites. Mr. Reed ate none.

Mrs. Butler would ask for updates when I returned each evening. My reply was always "The same. No better, no worse."

"Ben look all right?" she'd ask as she stitched another patch for a quilt. "You wait and see, Lizzie. My boy's gonna be a doctor someday. Just you wait and see."

"Yes, ma'am," I'd answer.

She'd smile and Mama would nod. But then, on Wednesday evening, they didn't get the chance to smile and nod. I didn't even get the chance to bring the boxed suppers to Mr. Reed's. Mrs. Butler was packing it up when the front door opened and clicked shut. The distinct shuffle of Ben's boots against the wood floor echoed through the house. The Wilkins couple, who'd been sitting at the kitchen table with Mama, looked at each other and grabbed up little Clara. They headed straight to their room.

In the quiet, it wasn't just Ben's boots that could be heard, but something else—something scratching and tapping against the floor and a heavy panting. Then, into the kitchen walked Ben, Ziggy trailing behind.

Ben looked at his ma. His eyes were swollen and red, his cheeks puffy. "Sit, Ziggy," he spoke. "You gotta mind me, 'cause you're my dog now."

Mrs. Butler ran over to Ben and wrapped her arms around him. She squeezed him tight. "It's all right, Ben. It was just his time, that's all. Mr. Reed lived a longer life than a lot of us."

Tears pooled up in my eyes, blurring the room and everybody in it. It was true. It wasn't fair. Ben shouldn't have to go through this again. Not Ben. He was too kind. Too good. Why him?

Mrs. Butler let go of Ben and pulled out a kitchen chair. She sat him down. He placed a crumpled piece of paper he'd been holding on the table and smoothed it.

"What's that?" Mama whispered.

"A poem. He told me to take it."

I figured a man as old as Mr. Reed had to be pretty wise. I figured if he thought this poem could help Ben, then maybe it could help us all. "Read it," I said.

Ben wiped his eyes on his shirtsleeve and nodded. He cleared his throat, then looked at me and said, " 'Wits' End Corner,' by Antoinette Wilson."

I smiled. Ben smiled back. And then he read slowly, softly:

> *"Are you standing at Wits' End Corner,*
> *Christian, with troubled brow?*
> *Are you thinking of what is before you,*
> *And all you are bearing now?*
> *Does all the world seem against you,*
> *And you in the battle alone?*
> *Remember—at Wits' End Corner*
> *Is just where God's power is shown.*
>
> *"Are you standing at Wits' End Corner,*
> *Blinded with wearying pain,*
> *Feeling you cannot endure it,*
> *You cannot bear the strain,*
> *Bruised through the constant suffering,*
> *Dizzy, and dazed, and numb?*
> *Remember—at Wits' End Corner*
> *Is where Jesus loves to come.*
>
> *"Are you standing at Wits' End Corner?*
> *Your work before you spread,*
> *All lying begun, unfinished,*

And pressing on heart and head,
Longing for strength to do it,
Stretching out trembling hands?
Remember—at Wits' End Corner
The Burden-Bearer stands.

"Are you standing at Wits' End Corner?
Then you're just in the very spot
To learn the wondrous resources
Of Him who faileth not:
No doubt to a brighter pathway
Your footsteps will soon be moved,
But only at Wits' End Corner
Is the God who is able proved."

I was right. Mr. Reed *was* wise. Wits' End Corner was the exact spot we'd all stood over the past year and a half. Mama reached up and took my hand. I looked down at her and I knew, just as Mr. Reed had known, that corner had finally been turned.

~ *Twenty-Two* ~

Misfortune Is a Good Teacher

Ben and I gathered up our poles and headed back to the house. Mid-September humidity hung heavy in the air, causing the sky to appear white instead of blue. Ol' One-Eye had eluded me once again, but I didn't mind. I guess he didn't like the feel of that hook jabbing through his mouth. Can't say I blamed him. Though I couldn't see him beneath the murky water, I saluted him, same as I had the day I caught him. He might've been just a slimy old catfish, but he was far smarter than me. It only took once for him to learn his lesson. Probably wasn't as stubborn as me.

"You can't catch One-Eye. You can't outshoot me with your slingshot. You've become an all-out loser, Lizzie Hawkins." Ben nudged me with his shoulder.

I nudged him back harder. "Have not. Least I'm not so ugly my cooties have to close their eyes."

Ben took a big gasp of air, pretending to be shocked that I'd say something as mean as that. But we both knew we were teasing. I wasn't an all-out loser—not yet, anyway. And I couldn't think of anybody who'd call Ben ugly. I watched him out of the corner of my eye trudging through the tall grass, his boots in his hands knocking against his knees as he went. It was good to have him near.

We'd spent this Sunday the way we'd spent most others since Mr. Reed had died: fishing and practicing with our slingshots. Sunday was the only day we both had the day off—me from Mr. Hinkle, him from Dr. Heimler.

After Mr. Reed passed, Dr. Heimler stopped by our house the very next day to check on Mama and the rest of us. He bragged on and on about Ben, saying he had all the promise in the world of becoming a doctor one day. I thought Mrs. Butler might faint. Next thing I knew, Dr. Heimler was offering Ben a job. He'd get the same pay as he had at Mr. Reed's, plus hands-on training for the job Mrs. Butler had always believed he'd someday hold. Best of all, when it was time to head to school the next morning, Ben had been with me. Education is mighty important to future doctors. "Dr. Benjamin Butler." Sounded good to me.

Mrs. Butler emerged onto the back porch. "Six o'clock, dinnertime. Better hurry in. Don't make me run behind."

Everybody knew not to mess with Mrs. Butler's schedule. Our four new boarders jumped up from the back porch rockers and darted inside. Only Mama remained. I waved. So did she.

"You know, boarders don't grate on me the way I thought they would," I said. "They're really kinda fun to have around. Well, mostly, anyway." I grabbed up a small rock and popped it into Ben's backside with my slingshot.

"Hey, what'd ya do that for?"

"A loser, huh? I'm a better shot than you think. I let you win, that's all."

"Sure," said Ben, his eyes crinkled up in a way that showed he wasn't sure at all.

Mrs. Butler's six Rhode Island Reds scattered across the backyard as we approached the house. They were allowed free range as long as they steered clear of Mama's vegetable garden.

We walked inside through the splintered back door, and as always, it was like entering a whole separate world. The soft whisper of the breeze grew into the low roar of chattering voices. A quilt Mrs. Butler and Mama had been working on hung from hooks attached to the parlor ceiling. Needles, colored threads, and scissors lay in a heap in its middle. All four bedrooms were full, and pallets of quilts and pillows were laid on the floor in the parlor each night. The youngest boarders liked those best—sleeping on a thick bed of quilts beneath the canopy of a soon-to-be quilt.

"No shooting people, Elizabeth Hawkins," said Mama, coming in behind us. She'd started talking more and more after Ben lost Mr. Reed. It was like Ben's loss woke something up inside of her, and she decided she was gonna be thankful for the people she had while she had 'em. With her fingers, she gently brushed hair off my sweaty forehead. "Remember, kindness is more persuasive than force."

Mrs. Butler added, "Or, you can catch more flies with honey than with vinegar."

Ben grinned at me. I knew what he was thinking. *Here we go again.* I suppose he thought I was thinking the same, but I wasn't.

"Yes, ma'am," I replied, wishing Mama had said that to me a whole lot sooner.

We all sat down to dinner, packed liked sardines around our table. Dinner was nothing but black-eyed peas and okra from our garden along with some dry corn bread on the side, but nobody seemed to mind.

I listened to the sharp clinking of spoons on plates and the low rumble of "please" and "thank you" being spoken and thought how lucky I was. For months I'd let fear and pride drive me, and it had nearly destroyed everything I loved. But once I let go of fear, life came much more easily. Dr. Heimler and I had even convinced Mama over the past months to slowly let go of her fear. She still wasn't her old self, but she now had a self. I hoped Erin would let go of her fear too. But she wasn't ready. Not yet.

That night I lay awake in bed.

Please, Lord, not again.

Sleep laughed at me, poked at me, refused to come. I rolled over and squinted at the clock, trying to make out the time. The soft white glow of moonlight lit its face. Ten till three. *Ugh!* It'd be another three hours before everyone else was up.

I'd been fighting all night. There wasn't any sense in whipping a dead horse. I eased out of the covers and tiptoed over to Mama's dresser. I pulled out my journal. Deep down I knew why sleep refused to come. There was something I still needed to let go. And so I did.

September 18, 1932

Dear Daddy,

They say when it rains in Alabama, it pours. I believe it. It poured on me all through 1931, straight on into 1932. It was then that I lost something I never thought I would. It wasn't a locket, my grades, or a friend. It wasn't money or pride, though I lost those things too. It was you.

It wasn't death that took you from me. Maybe it would've been easier if it had. While I don't have to face the death of your body, I must face the death of your spirit. A person I'd always believed to be strong and brave has proved weak and cowardly. But the loss of you, my daddy, wasn't where my story ended; it's where it began. In losing you I found myself. For that I'm grateful and, most of all, proud.

I've succeeded at the number one most important thing you ever taught me—I played the

terrible cards I was dealt; I turned some mighty
sour lemons into lemonade; I worked with what
I had, and what I had sure wasn't much. I hope
wherever you are, you're proud of me too, not
because of grades, or a blue ribbon, or a fish, but
because I conquered the things you were too afraid
to fight. You were too afraid to fail.

I'm letting go of any hope that you'll ever come
home. As life unfolds a path before me, I'll walk
it with those who fill our home with smiles and
love each day. But I know you won't be here to
walk beside me. You chose a different path, a path
I couldn't follow. And yes, I'm still too stubborn
to try.

Yep, like they always say, when it rains, it
pours. But I hope, at least here in the South, that
when the sun finally decides to shine, it beams.

> *Love always,*
> *Your Lizzie Girl*

I laid my pencil on the dresser and read over what I'd written. It was truth—love-it-or-hate-it truth.

I flipped through the pages past my newest entry. There were many empty ones left, but the day would come when they'd be empty no more.

I closed the journal, placed it in the drawer, and crawled back into bed beside Mama. I slipped beneath the soft sheets. In the morning I'd pull out Daddy's good-bye note. I'd leave it folded; then I'd rip it apart and throw it away. I didn't need to read it now. I wouldn't need to read it ever again.

I curled up and closed my eyes. For the first time since Daddy had gone, sleep came easy and deep, bringing with it a dream.

Author's Note

While Lizzie's story is a fictional one, it was inspired by stories told to me and my family by my paternal grandmother, Nelda Posey Perry. After losing her mother at the age of twelve, she was left with a strict father who expected her to take on many responsibilities—cooking, cleaning, and caring for younger siblings. I've often wondered what that must've been like for her. Like me, she was a self-admitted dreamer. Like Lizzie, she was highly spirited. I feel that through Lizzie, a part of her lives on.

If Lizzie's spirit belongs to my paternal grandmother, then Ben's heart is my paternal grandfather's. Like Ben, my grandfather dropped out of school to help support his family. He had not yet completed seventh grade when he went to work at a local mine. Unlike Ben, he never went back to school.

This was not uncommon for children growing up during the Great Depression. Mr. James Hubbard, a family friend, also temporarily left school to help out around the family farm. He was given the responsibility of plowing the field. His father showed him how to do it, then left him alone to get it done. Mr. Hubbard was nervous, but he plowed onward—right over his big toe! As did Ben's, Mr. Hubbard's big toenail came off. He went to find his father and have a good cry. His father instructed him to man up and get back to plowing. He did.

Stories of kids being forced to grow up quickly during the 1930s seem endless. My husband's paternal grandmother, Helen Bryant Golden, also lost her mother at a young age. She too was expected to cook for her family, and the first-try rock-hard biscuits Lizzie describes could have been Nanny Golden's own. In real life, Nanny's older brothers laughed at her. But she got the last laugh—her biscuits certainly are not rock hard anymore.

Fortunately, none of these people ever had to awaken one morning and discover that their father had left, though that was a shock many did endure. During the 1930s, men were considered their families' breadwinners. When the stock market crashed in 1929, millions of men lost their jobs and were unable to find reemployment. Like Lizzie's daddy, many fell into despair, feeling ashamed and humiliated that they could no longer provide for their families. Unable to bear the guilt, some men simply ran away. By 1940, 1.5 million men had abandoned their families.

In *Every Day After*, Mama becomes terribly depressed and withdrawn when Daddy disappears. Lizzie refuses to let Dr. Heimler examine Mama for fear that he'll send her off to the hospital or mental ward. Lizzie had good reason to be afraid. Beginning in the mid-1800s and continuing well beyond the 1930s, people exhibiting signs of mental illness were typically institutionalized. These patients were afflicted with maladies ranging from severe depression (like Mama) to epilepsy (like me) and were often mistreated.

The mentally ill weren't the only unfortunates sent to state institutions. Children regularly ended up in grossly overcrowded orphanages. Parents struggling to feed and provide for their children opted to place them in state care with the intention of taking them back when times improved. Sadly for some of those children, their parents never returned.

When orphanages ran out of room, children were sent into foster care. Since people struggled so desperately with finances during this era, many families agreed to take in orphans just to receive money from the state. When foster parents tired of their responsibilities, the luckless children were sent back to the orphanage to await yet another foster home. Orphans were usually tossed hither and yon, unable to enjoy a stable, nurturing upbringing. Some ran away, choosing instead a life of hopping trains and begging for food.

I imagine that those children, along with most everyone forced to survive the harshness of the Depression, truly felt at their wits' end, and when I first read the poem "Wits' End Corner" by Antoinette Wilson, I knew I wanted to include it in the story. It sums up the despair folks must have felt during the 1930s, yet it conveys a great sense of hope.

Finally, Mama's treasured book of proverbs is real. As Lizzie would say, it holds bragging rights for being·one of the longest titles I have ever laid eyes on: *Curiosities in Proverbs: A Collection of Unusual Adages, Maxims, Aphorisms, Phrases and Other Popular Dicta from Many Lands*. Whew! It was published in 1916 and was arranged with annotations by Dwight Edwards Marvin. Most of the chapter titles in *Every Day After* are proverbs taken from this book.

Acknowledgments

The people I wish to thank are few, but they each played an indispensible role in the development and publication of this book. You know what they say: quality over quantity. I am extremely blessed by the quality of people who surround me every day.

First, to my husband, Michael. Without you, Lizzie's story might never have been told. You have been my biggest cheerleader and my biggest fan since day one. Thank you for believing in me and for pushing me forward when everyone else, including me, thought I should turn back. This journey wouldn't have been the same without you.

I struck editor gold with Michelle Poploff. Thank you, Michelle, for your wisdom, your insight, and your guidance. Your willingness to shepherd debut authors reminds me of another editor with the initials M.P.—the late, legendary Maxwell Perkins.

A thousand thanks to retired publisher Bud Flora and his gracious wife, Georgia, for taking the time to read an early draft of the manuscript and for your fervent insistence that it had potential. Most of all, thank you for your friendship.

A million thanks to my parents, Mark and Jackie Perry. Thank you, Mama, for reading version after version of the story, and thank you, Daddy, for celebrating with me when the good news finally arrived. You both mean more to me than you know.

This story would not have turned out the same without the personal experiences of the following: my late paternal grandparents, Jake and Nelda Perry; my husband's paternal grandparents, Helen and John Golden; my maternal grandmother, Sue Lively; and Mr. James Hubbard. Thank you all for sharing your memories with me.

A heartfelt thanks to Chris and Ray Pelham for being kind enough to sift through old family photos with me.

To my two boys, Cade and Tanner, thank you for allowing me to take over the computer and for keeping my life interesting. I love you both!

And finally, because they are forced to put up with me, a big thanks to my sister and brother, Rebecca and Griff. You guys are the best.

About the Author

As a child, Laura Golden was a reader, a dreamer, and a listener. She loved to read everything from cereal boxes to C. S. Lewis (still does); she loved to dream of becoming everything from a figure skater to a fairy-tale princess (still does, but don't tell anyone); and she loved to listen to older generations spin tales about the "good ol' days" (still does, and she's always willing to lend an ear).

Laura lives with her husband and two sons on a lovely piece of Alabama countryside just east of Birmingham. This is her first (but hopefully not her last) novel.